TWINKL...

A Marlow and Sage Mystery

LEE STRAUSS

Twinkle Little Star

By Lee Strauss

Cover by Steven Novak Illustrations

Copyright © 2016

La Plume Press

www.laplumepress.com

ISBN: 978-1988677002

Chapter One

SAGE

I'VE DONE a lot of stupid things in my life. Most of them in the last year and a half since I registered for classes at Detroit University. Running for a seat on the student government council was my latest one. What was I thinking? Maybe that it would look good on my resume? Maybe that it would help me recover from the social drop I'd inexplicably experienced this last year.

"You can't beat me, you know."

Stella Flowers, brunette, hour-glass figure, head cheerleader, and over-confident snob, watched me from behind her table. She stood tall, head cocked, lips pursed with a hand firmly on one bony hip.

"Maybe I can, maybe I can't."

That was my best response? I groaned inwardly. I deserved to lose to her. Moving around my table, the standard school issue kind with metal legs and a faux wood-grain top, I handed out small flyers to students who meandered through the large lobby of the student resource building. It had high ceilings and tall windows that cast long streams of light. The floors were brown subway tiles and between them and the height of the room, it created an echo chamber effect. I could hear snippets of conversation from across the way.

"Vote for Sage Farrell," I said with feigned confidence. My flyers had my yearbook picture, slightly grainy with a strained smile, and bullet points as to why I should be elected for the sophomore representative over Stella Flowers:

- conscientious
- hard-working
- people-person

With this splashy slogan: *You talk—I listen*

Stella stepped into the crowd in front of me and handed out larger flyers, pink actually, with the bold message, "Vote for Stella!"

Apparently she was so popular, she didn't need a last name.

She also had an assistant, her sidekick Minji Park. I'd met Minji before. She used to share a room with

Zed's crazy old-girlfriend. Minji had a shiny black bob and dark brown eyes, was cute and sweet, but she withered under Stella's flamboyant personality. I wondered how Stella had gotten her claws into her.

I had to concede that it would be nice to have an assistant. My heart contracted at the thought of my best-friend Teagan who'd passed away the year before. If she were here, she'd be helping me. She was an artist so she would've made me great posters and my table display would be fit for a show-room window rather than being the sorry blank canvas that it was. Teagan would've gushed her belief in me to everyone she knew. I missed her.

Stella stage-whispered to Minji, "Get me a bottle of water."

Minji's shoulders slumped and she shuffled away to do Stella's bidding.

I continued my efforts to distribute flyers and talk to people, most of who waved me off and kept walking. My head jerked toward the sound of Stella's high-pitched laugh. A small crowd had gathered around her. Was she actually signing autographs? Seriously?

Then I spotted Marlow Henry. He was another stupid thing I had done, or rather hadn't done. With my head in a cloud of conceit, I'd repeatedly pursued the wrong type of bad news guy while Marlow, an actual awesome guy, was right there, waiting for me.

Until he wasn't. Every guy has his limits, and suddenly he had a pretty, petite, pink-haired girlfriend. You know how they say, *You don't know what you have until it's gone?* So true. Marlow and Dakota looked adorable as they chatted and I watched them from across the lobby with a sense of regret.

Marlow and I had been through some crazy times together over the last year. Always just as friends. It'd been a while since something bizarre had pulled us together, and the fact was, now that he was attached, we rarely spent time with each other. When we did manage to be in the same room, conversation was stilted and uncomfortable.

Minji came back with Stella's water and took over the job of handing out her flyers. Stella returned to her seat behind her table just as a gorgeous guy claimed Minji's empty chair. He hugged Stella's neck and gave her a long passionate kiss.

Of course I knew who he was; all the girls at DU did—Wyatt Banks, a good-looking junior in the advanced track, the only son of a powerful political family. He wore his dark hair shaved close on the sides and longer on top, with a half-inch-long beard that covered the lower part of a ruddy, lightly freckled face.

Not that I noticed.

I sighed. Stella definitely had all the advantages. Popularity, an assistant, a boyfriend.

But even though Wyatt's hand massaged Stella's neck, his hazel eyes peered over her shoulder and landed on me. He smiled crookedly as his gaze scanned me from head to toe and back, finishing their trek with a wink.

I didn't smile back.

Another guy meandered through the thinning crowd, one of the science geeks that hung out with Zed and Marlow. Brandt something. He hovered around Stella's well-presented table, but his eyes, with a look that flashed with a mix of both fear and affection, were locked on Minji. I noted how he kept back from Minji's peripheral vision, so she wouldn't notice him looking. I wondered if she knew she had an admirer.

I glanced back at Marlow and Dakota in time to see them kiss quickly and part ways. Dakota strolled in my direction.

I had an idea—probably another stupid one. On impulse, I jogged impulsively toward Dakota and tapped her arm. She looked up at me with wary eyes. I smiled to reassure her.

"Hey, I'm wondering if you'd like to help me with my campaign? If you have time." Her brows furrowed and I added quickly. "It'll look good on your resume."

"Why me?" she asked.

"Because we're friends, aren't we? And Marlow is

my friend and your boyfriend, so we have him in common."

Dakota frowned and I knew I'd said the wrong thing. One thing Dakota didn't want to do was share Marlow with me in any way.

But then she surprised me by saying, "Okay. I'll do it. Do you need help now?"

I nodded and led her back to my table, wondering if we were both thinking the same thing: Keep your friends close, but your enemies closer.

Chapter Two

CRYSTAL

CRYSTAL MORRISETTE ADDED another layer of fire engine-red lipstick to her gel-infused lips and smacked them together. Her newly-dyed hair shimmered like a bonfire in the bathroom light. She'd been a blond for the last three months, but with profile views waning she had to do something— nothing like a change in hair color to stir up new interest!

She tugged down her black tankini—one size too small, forcing her assets up and out. These were the money shots—cleavage plus puckered red lips. Crystal stretched out her arm and tilted the phone until her image filled the screen. She clicked the button, quickly examined the image, then frowned.

She looked like a duck.

Retake.

The image was blurry.

Retake.

Her arm tired.

Retake.

The lighting was wrong, casting shadows under her eyes. Damn—she looked thirty years old!

Retake.

Crystal moved to her bedroom and opened the curtains, letting natural light into the cramped space. Traffic moved briskly along the street, and she watched a guy with dark hair swept over his forehead enter the pawn shop underneath her apartment. Crystal was familiar with most of Lambert's customers, but she hadn't seen this one before.

He must have felt her staring because he glanced up and caught her eye. Crystal smiled at him, because that was what she did with men. *Smile, smile, smile.*

The guy froze, and stared like he'd never seen a pretty girl before. He wasn't scrawny or anything, but his face was unremarkable. Square. Squinty eyes half-hidden by windblown fringe.

Crystal finger-waved and stepped out of the man's view before he could respond. She dodged piles of discarded clothing that littered the floor, and positioned herself once again in front of the mirror. It took twelve tries, but she finally got a shot she could post.

With five million followers, Crystal could sell

caption space to advertisers—lingerie and cosmetic companies, mostly. Today it was the hair product brand that she used to change her hair color. On a good day, she could make three hundred dollars from a single post. Three hundred bucks!

She was hoping for a good day.

#newhair #redheadsrule #endofsummer #stepinto-fall #autumncolors

There was nothing quite as exhilarating as uploading a new photo and watching for follower engagement.

Crystal practiced her poses while she waited. Hmm. Slow day. Usually she got responses within seconds praising her beauty and her bravery. Finally a comment:

"So sick of seeing your ugly mug!"

Then another.

"Get a life, loser."

Crystal scowled. Dumb trolls. Jealous middle-aged women, probably. That didn't stop her stomach from twisting with a new surge of anxiety. She wasn't getting any younger. How long before she's a has-been?

Then the good ones rolled in.

"Hey beautiful!"

"You are so gorgeous."

"Can I have your number?"

Crystal finally smiled. See? The people loved her! Most of them, anyway.

Still, she wasn't getting the comment frenzy she once had. Not even with the change of hair color. She clicked over to her competition—Violet Vee, from Chicago. Detroit and Chicago were natural competitors in everything from sports to tourism to who got the most snowfall. Social media starlets were no different.

Starlet wasn't her word. A fan had called her that. Crystal liked it. Starlet to actual Star - that was her plan. She was saving her money to go to Hollywood next summer.

Violet Vee had posted recently too. But wait. What was going on with her numbers? Look at all the comments and likes! This couldn't be happening. Violet Vee's post wasn't anything special. Same hair. Same body. She was taller than Crystal, but Crystal had the curves.

Crystal's gut churned anew. If she didn't beat out Violet Vee, she might lose her sponsors. She gripped one of her many crystal figurines—this one an owl—between her manicured fingers. She'd bought the first few as a gimmick, a play on her name, and before long her fans were mailing them to her. Dozens and dozens. Her apartment was filled with tiny, sparkling animals, astronomy symbols, and fantasy characters. She paced back and forth in a small area free of shoes and other sundry items as she pressed the owl to her lips. *Think, think, think.* She had to do something. Something more than a shot of her breasts and her hair. Some kind of stunt. Something outrageous to get the people talking about her.

She let out a defeated sigh. Despite her growing anxiety and desperation, her mind drew a blank.

Chapter Three

MARLOW

I'D BEEN RUINED for the ordinary.

Half-way through the first semester of my sopho-more year at Detroit University, even with a full course load in science and math, I actually felt kind of bored. After the crazy, and I admit, exciting things that happened with Sage Farrell over the last year, I was finding it hard to accept life as a regular student. A regular guy.

I spotted Sage across the foyer in the student build-ing. I was careful not to let Dakota catch me stealing glances. There was something about Sage that called to me. She looked tired. Vulnerable, without her usual spunk. Still beautiful though, with her long dark hair pulled back in a wavy ponytail that shimmered under the florescent lights.

Snap out of it, Henry!

I was with Dakota not Sage, and if I was going to think about a girl, it had to be the one with *pink* hair.

Fall in Detroit could be chilly, and the October landscape was filled with half-naked trees that shivered under lingering drizzle. The skies were gray and dismal, with only the red brick of the campus buildings adding color to the gloom.

I pressed into the biting wind, tightening my arms against my chest. Another month and my nose hairs would start freezing. Note to self: don't let short girlfriend see frozen nostril hairs.

Finally arriving at my dorm I welcomed the blast of warm, slightly smelly, testosterone-filtered air.

I shared a room with my best friend Zed Zabinsky. His first name was Arnold but nobody called him that. His nickname Zed was a nod to his Canadian roots. He and I have been best friends since grade school. We went through all the dorky, awkward years together—a phase that only just started to diminish minimally last year. Zed didn't have a girlfriend currently—I told him he should shave that scruffy beard—but he hung out with Dakota and me a lot. Too much in my opinion, but hey, I wasn't the kind of guy to ditch his best friend for a girl.

They were assigned according to the kind of faculty you were part of, so all the guys in this building

were in some sort of math and/or science track, from
Freshmen to Senior.

Zed and I co-existed in a little closet-sized room
where I could stretch my leg out and touch his bed. I
tossed my jacket on the foot of my bed and dropped
into my desk chair. I needed to study for a midterm
exam in physics, which was my major. The door to the
hall stood open, I'd forgotten to close it when I came in,
and I could see into the common area where the guys
gathered to play video games as they sat on the old
couch in the corner or hung out in the kitchenette-type
space along the opposite wall to make bad pots of
coffee.

Today several of the guys huddled together in the
middle of the room including the geek brothers who
weren't really brothers, Steve and Paul were a nerdy
version of Simon and Garfunkel, minus the talent. I
could see Wyatt Banks with his head of hair swooped
off his forehead, and Zed, who'd just blustered in from
the cold, joining them. Curiosity got the better of me
and I dropped my textbooks and sauntered over and
stood beside Harland Payne, a senior.

"What's up?" I said.

Zed stepped sideways to let me in the circle where
Wyatt Banks held his iPad for all of us to see. I let out
a sigh, not sure why I was surprised. On the screen
was a photo of a half-naked girl looking over a pearly

white shoulder and smiling with bright red lips. Same old, same old, but these guys were enamored by the image.

Except apparently, for Brandt Rheinhold. "She's not as hot as she used to be."

Wyatt protested. "Are you kidding me man? She's a babe. Totally hot I'm in *love*."

Isaac Cavanaugh punched him in the arm. "Dude, you have a girlfriend."

"Who is she?" I asked.

Isaac's head swiveled to me in astonishment. "You don't know who Crystal Morrisette is?"

I took another look at the image on the screen. "I guess she does look familiar."

Steve laughed. "Man, you've had that little girl-friend for too long."

Paul snickered, agreeing. "Crystal Morrisette is da bomb."

I prickled at that. "What's so special about this one? She's just another pretty girl."

"That may be," Isaac said, "but this one has five million followers on Instagram. She's a media star. Like a Detroit Kardashian."

I lifted a shoulder, not caring in the least.

"Don't tell me you don't know who the Kardashians are?" Paul said loudly. Seemed there was always a good time to mock someone.

Steve snorted in my defense. "At least he has an actual girlfriend. You can't kiss Crystal Morrisette."

"Oh yeah?" Paul said. "Watch this." He snatched Wyatt's iPad and smacked his lips against the dirty screen to a chorus of riotous laughter.

Chapter Four

HE'D ANSWERED AN AD: Shed for rent—private location— for storage or other use.

The property, which had a pawn shop on it as well, wasn't far from Detroit University campus—a definite bonus—and the rent was reasonable. Lambert, the plump and friendly old man of Lambert's Pawn Shop showed him the unit. Pale blue paint chipped off the graying weather worn wood exterior, but the inside was in decent shape. Plain walls painted white, vinyl flooring that looked like oak hardwood. A simple arrangement of sink, fridge and hotplate.

"My nephew needed a place to crash for awhile," Lambert explained. "He renovated in exchange for rent. Put in that kitchenette."

The nephew had left a kitchen table with two

chairs and a six-foot long plush sofa dotted with dusty stains.

The shed was tucked in behind the shop across the narrow driveway. Mature landscaping, hedges and bushes blocked the view of the shed from most of Lambert's neighbors.

"A single gal rents the apartment above the store," Lambert explained. "But she's a good tenant, quiet. I never see her."

That was the only glitch. He glanced up at the apartment. Exterior steps led to a door painted bright red. He'd caught the tenant staring at him when he strolled up to the pawn shop entrance. She was pretty. Sort of familiar, but he couldn't place her. Maybe a student at DU? Unfortunately the back of her apartment had a perfect view of the shed. She could be trouble.

Lambert wanted cash under the table, so the price was great and the location was perfect. He didn't think he'd find anything else on short notice and he was eager to get started. He was sure he could handle one silly girl.

He smiled at Lambert. "I'll take it."

It only took him a couple days to get it set up. Computers, monitors, electrical boards, standard lab equipment. Electronics parts he bought from Lambert. His work consumed him and he'd completely forgotten about the girl next door, so when she appeared, seemingly out of nowhere, he jumped, like he'd seen a ghost.

Because he *knew* this girl. Every red-blooded guy in Michigan knew her. He remembered now why she looked familiar. He followed her on Instagram! She wore more make-up and less clothing there, so that was why he hadn't caught on right away.

"Hey," she called out.

He stopped mid-stride, just steps away from the shed and stared at her in a way that made him feel guilty, like he didn't have a right to be in her yard. He was mesmerized by the sight of her not on a screen but in the flesh, exotic and dangerous, like spotting a panther in the wild.

"What are you doing?" she asked, stepping toward him. She wore a white down jacket and skin-tight blue jeans. Her unnaturally red hair flowed out from under a pink wool hat and she wore black gloves that were wrapped around a smoothie. Pouty lips sucked on the straw, causing him further distraction and unwanted physical response.

"I'm renting the shed from Lambert."

"Really? For what?"

"Nothing. Just... stuff."

She tossed the empty drink container into a nearby trash can and removed her gloves, slipping them into her pockets. "Just stuff? Let me guess. You're gonna grow weed."

"N-no," he stammered. "Nothing like that."

She smiled coyly. "Then what?"

"Just setting up a lab. For science."

"No way!" She said, amping up her smile. "Cute *and* smart."

His mouth dropped open, his eyes blinking. Had she seriously called him cute? No one has ever called him that, at least not to his face. Not even his own mother. The girl seemed unaware of how her friendly approach was making his insides turn to mush. She continued like the earth hadn't just flipped on its axis.

"So, what kind of science?"

"Physics. Quantum. Quantum physics."

"Wow. Well maybe someday you can show me your secrets." She winked seductively and he flushed red. She added a wiggle to her walk as she left him, and shouted over her shoulder as she skipped up the steps to her door.

"Check me out on Instagram," she called over her shoulder as she skipped up the steps to her door. "Crystal Morrisette!"

"I will!" he shouted. "I mean. I am. I already follow you!"

Ugh. What a loser. *I already follow you?*

Chapter Five

SAGE

I HAD A NEW BOY TOY.

Mechanical this time. A lovely, slightly rusty, cherry red 1996 Toyota pickup truck. Low-riding, no extended cab. Could squeeze in two passengers if the middle person was small. After the fiasco with my former bosses last summer I took the last pay checks I'd gotten from them and bought this beauty. Since I had no boyfriend, and the guy I liked was with another girl, I felt that Boy Toy and I deserved each other.

My brother was busy with his own girlfriend, Janelle. She lived in the same dorm building I did, so at least I saw my brother once in a while, even though he was never there to hang out with me. My roommate Nora O'Shea was still with her boyfriend Jake, so for the first time in a long time, I was alone without best friend or boyfriend. Teagan's absence left a deep hole in my heart and I didn't think I'd ever fully recover from losing her. But Boy Toy helped.

My fingers tapped on the steering wheel to a country tune on the stereo as I drove from the city of Detroit to the university campus across the river. I loved the feeling of independence and freedom I had while driving. Gas and insurance was a kicker to my pocket book, but totally worth it.

I pulled into the parking lot behind my dorm and the engine cut out with a sputter. "It's okay, Boy, we're here now. You can rest." There were a lot of miles on Boy Toy's engine, and I had to go easy on him. It wasn't like I had any where to go besides school, and my parents' house. Mom and Dad worried that I had spent too much money on something I didn't need, but my brother was relieved, because now I'd stop asking to borrow his car.

Nora was in our room when I arrived. She was creating a complicated braid in her long red hair that could compete with any of the hairdos on Game of Thrones.

"Oh good, you're back," she said. "You can come with me to watch Jake's hockey practice, and after that drinks."

My top lip snarled up into my best Elvis impersonation. "That's not really my scene."

She snapped the final elastic to her hair master-piece and locked her hazel gaze on me. "Your scene is wherever the single guys are hanging out, my friend. And this is where they're hanging out."

I shrugged. "I'm not really up to it."

"Seriously, Sage. It's time to stop sulking. You're a killjoy these days. I know you had a couple hard blows recently. I don't deny that. But it's time for you to shake it off, make a new start."

I couldn't decide if I should be offended by her callousness or feel blessed to have a friend who seem-ingly cared about me. I *had* been a lot more solemn and moody these days. And I used to be very social. A real butterfly. I missed being social. The old me was social. It used to be *me* cajoling Teagan to go out when she didn't want to. Even though I'd rather curl up in a ball under my covers and read a book, I heard myself say, "Okay, I'll come."

We bundled up in sweaters and wool hats and knitted scarfs like it was the middle of December instead of late October. Not only was it chilly outside, the arena was freezing. There was something off about seeing your breath when you were inside a building.

We'd only just sat down on one of the bleachers when Nora nudged me gently and pointed. "What about that guy?

"Who?"

"Number eight. His name is Isaac. He's nice. And as far as I know he's unattached."

I squinted, but it was hard to see his face from this distance. He had a strong slap shot and filled out his practice uniform nicely.

After the scrimmage, Nora talked me into going out for beer and burgers. We were joined by Jake his friend Chet and a couple other girls who were apparently also on the lookout for single guys.

Somehow Nora maneuvered the seating arrangement so that I ended up sitting beside Number Eight. "Isaac, meet my roommate, Sage," she announced loudly, Then she leaned down to whisper in my ear, "Don't forget to smile." I shot her a dirty look.

We were joined by Jake and his friend Chet, a guy I knew casually, but didn't really know, and by a couple other girls who were apparently also on the look out for single guys.

There was an awkward moment of silence and I could almost see the wheels in Isaac's head spinning, trying to come up with something to say to me. Finally he said, "Have we met before?"

"I don't think so."

He broke into a toothy smile. "I remember! You used to date that guy Tristan Coy, right?"

I leaned back. "Don't remind me."

Isaac looked stricken.

"It's okay," I added quickly. "He's just not my favorite topic."

Two empty chairs across from us were claimed by none other than Stella Flowers and Wyatt Banks. I suppressed a groan. I really wasn't in the mood for Stella and her perky ambition. She ignored me as she wrestled out of her jacket. Wyatt and Isaac greeted each other with a fist bump across the table.

Wyatt chin nodded my way and gave Isaac a thumbs up, like Isaac had completed a difficult quest by sitting by me.

I thought Nora had taken the chair to my left, but when I turned to mutter a complaint I found her oaf of a boyfriend, Jake, was there instead. This night was going downhill fast.

"Hey, Sage," he grunted. Then he turned his back on me.

The server arrived and we ordered pizza and beer. I expected talk to be about hockey and sports and game stats and who the MVPs were, but to my surprise, part way through, Wyatt and Isaac started discussing the New Scientist Innovation Award contest.

"You guys are into science?" I couldn't keep the surprise out of my voice.

"You don't have to look like a nerd to be smart," Wyatt said.

"No, I know. Just, good for you."

Stella draped a slender arm around Wyatt's neck and smirked at me. "He's not just eye candy."

I ignored her. "Are you guys going to enter?"

Wyatt glanced at Isaac then said, "The winner gets full scholarship to a master degree program and a bonus five thousand bucks to invest in development. So, yeah."

"So what's your experiment?"

Wyatt chuckled. "We can't tell you. No offense. We can't really tell anyone."

Isaac added, "We could have the winning idea. Can't risk it getting stolen."

"That wouldn't really happen would it?" I said.

Wyatt's eyes darkened in a serious stare. "With this kind of publicity, and the doors it would open, you better believe it."

The conversation abruptly changed to beer—which was best Budweiser, or Bud Lite?—and I couldn't help but suppress a yawn. I'd had enough.

Just as I was reaching for my purse to leave, my phone buzzed. It was a text message. From Wyatt asking me if I wanted to go out sometime.

I shot him a withering look. He sat across from me with a cocky grin on his face while sitting right next to Stella! The nerve.

Chapter Six

CRYSTAL

CRYSTAL'S tiny kitchen window faced the alley, a perfect spot for her to spy on her interesting new neighbor. Fringe wasn't a talker and seemed to rush in and out, his gaze darting up to her door, as if he were afraid of being seen by her, or worse, cornered and forced into another conversation. He spent most weekends and some evenings in the shed. To say she was curious about what he was doing in there was an understatement. She was curious by nature—some would call her a snoop. She didn't apologize for it. Information was power. She'd do anything to get to the top and stay there. Anything.

Crystal took a sip from her glass of wine and stared out the window, the dust and grime suddenly an irritant. Setting the wine glass down on the narrow counter, she rummaged under the sink retrieving glass cleaner and paper towel. She spritzed and wiped, and she was almost finished the task when her eye caught sight of a blinding flash of light coming from inside the shed.

What was that? Was Fringe all right? Had he electrocuted himself with his science stuff?

Crystal dropped the cleaner into the sink, grabbed her jacket and rushed outside and down the stairs, gasping a little at the brittlely cold air. A rumbling noise filtered through Fringe's door, masking the sound of her knuckles rapping against it. She wanted to call out, but realized she didn't know the guy's name. She always referred to him in her mind as Fringe, even after he showed up last week with a hair cut.

"Hello!" Crystal knocked harder. "Are you okay?"

When the door remained unanswered, she dragged over an empty wooden crate from Lambert's heap of junk leaning up against the shed and she positioned it under the window next to a large bush. She wasn't sure what she thought she'd see—maybe Fringe's body lying limply on the floor—but not *this*. If she hadn't seen it with her own eyes, she never would have believed it. It was impossible, but...

Her knees felt weak and she almost stumbled off the crate.

This was crazy. How many other people knew

about Fringe's experiment? None if she could go by the number of people he'd brought to the shed. Crystal would've noticed if Fringe had company.

But now *she* knew. And it gave her an idea. A sly smile crossed her face as she sprinted back to the warmth of her apartment.

Fringe had become her new obsession.

No one had moved the crate tucked in beside the bush underneath the shed window, and Crystal took that as a sign from the universe. Dressing in dark colors with a mug of coffee for warmth, she took her position on the box. She could see through the bush's branches, yet they worked to hide her.

It was important that Fringe didn't discover how much she knew about him. That she knew his schedule. Mondays, Wednesdays and Fridays from 8:00 p.m. to midnight; weekends 11:00 a.m. to 6:00 p.m., only taking one short break to grab a sub sandwich around noon, and early Tuesday and Thursday mornings from 5:00 to 7:00. She'd discovered this by accident, having gotten up one Tuesday morning just before five to use the bathroom, and then again on a Thursday at seven in time to see Fringe leave.

On Sunday Crystal decided she was ready to move on to the next stage of her plan. She had no doubt Fringe would give her what she wanted. Blackmail combined with seduction was a convincing and intoxicating elixir - a magic potion she would serve to Fringe.

After a short time spent spying on Fringe through the window, she stepped off the crate, ran fingers through her hair and popped a mint into her mouth. She took a moment to add a bit of gloss to her lips—she always carried a lip product in her pocket—then rapped her knuckles on the door.

The humming sound that she had grown accustomed to went silent. She knocked again, harder this time. A few seconds later the door cracked open and Fringe stuck out his stubby nose, keeping the door tight around his body so that she couldn't see inside.

"Yeah?"

"Hey, you want to hang out?" Crystal batted her eyelashes and slowly ran her thumb nail along her bottom lip. It had the desired effect. Fringe's jaw dropped and he stared mesmerized at her mouth. It took him a few seconds to regain his composure. He straightened his broad shoulders and stared down at her.

"I'm kind of busy."

"Yeah, I know," she said this with a conspiratorial

wink. "I have to confess, I've been a Peeping Tom. Or shall I say a Peeping Sally."

Fringe seemed to blanch at that.

"Hey don't worry." Crystal nudged up to Fringe and pressed her hand against his chest, forcing him to take a small step back. "Your secret is safe with me." She ran her fingers along his bare arm until they reached his palm and laced her fingers through his, then drew him back inside the shed and closed the door.

Chapter Seven

SAGE

I ANSWERED a rap at my door and was startled to find my brother Ben standing in the hallway. He was alone, without his girlfriend Janelle.

"Hey," I said. "What's up?"

Ben shoved his fists into his pockets and sauntered in. As I closed the door behind him, he sat casually on my desk chair, causing it to sink under his bulky weight. There was a reason why he'd been a star football player—he was born with the wide shoulders and physical mass of a linebacker. He still wore his team jersey.

Ben gave a cursory glance at the mess on Nora's side of the room. She reminded me of a human tornado. Her clothing draped over every free surface on her side. Not a single drawer of her dresser was closed and personal items flowed out of the drawers like it was a lingerie waterfall. I liked tidiness and found a sense of peace when things were organized and put away. My bed was made, my drawers closed, my fashion frames arranged neatly on a tray. My closet doors closed all the way. We were like the odd couple, our room a before and after photo shoot illustration of an explosion at American Apparel.

Turning his back on Nora's disaster, Ben rested his elbows on his knees, put his chin on his hands and looked at me with worried eyes. I'd seen this look so many times growing up. It was what he would do when he had a dilemma, whether at school with teachers or with his friends or his teammates, and often with his girlfriend-of-the-month.

I hopped onto my bed, folded my legs yoga style, and leaned forward. "Spill."

"I want to leave Detroit."

I jerked back, sincerely surprised. We were both raised in Detroit by our adoptive parents. It wasn't paradise for sure, but it was home.

"Really? Why? Where do you want to go?"

He let out a tired sigh. "I'm restless. I need to travel. I saved up money over the summer and I want to see the world. I haven't decided yet what I want to do with my life, what to pursue for a career, but I think maybe I'll figure it out if I go on a trip."

I felt a little jealous. "That sounds exciting. Do you have an idea where you'll go?"

"I thought I'd start with New York, then fly to England, France, Germany, Switzerland over to the Eastern countries like Hungary and Romania, and then make my way south through Africa. From South Africa I'd head to Malaysia, Australia and then back to LA. I figure by the time I get to California I'll know what the hell I want to do with my life."

Now I was really jealous. "Wow. That's quite the itinerary."

"You can get a pretty good deal for around-the-world travel if you go one direction, especially if you're a student."

I filed that away for future reference. "How long would it take?"

"Six to nine months, probably."

I was beginning to suspect the problem. "That's a long time to be away from Janelle."

"I know it's a long time, and I expect to be a changed man when I get back. I won't be the same person as I am now. And I'd don't expect her to wait for me. I just don't know if it's fair for me to stay with her now, even though I'm not planning to leave until the new year."

I unfolded my legs and dropped back onto my

pillow, considering. "Have you talked to her about this?"

Ben huffed. "You don't know Janelle that well do you? She'll freak out. Like *really*. She's already planning our wedding."

"No way! Please tell me you haven't proposed!" That would make his decision significantly more tricky.

"No, *no*. Of course not. I can just tell by the things she says and the hints she drops that she's expecting a future with me. That this is a long-term relationship in her mind."

"But not in yours?"

"There was a time when I thought maybe she could be the one. But the fact that I'm willing to leave her behind for half a year to find myself is pretty telling isn't it?"

I nodded. "Yes it is. It sounds like you already know what you have to do."

Ben shifted backward, his legs stretching out long, and he tipped his chin up to the ceiling. "I just hate that I'm going to hurt her."

This was what I loved about my brother. He was one of the good ones. Not a jerk like all the guys I seemed to be attracted to. Well, all the guys except for Marlow.

Ben rubbed his face and got to his feet. "I'll do it

next week. She's so excited about the bush party this weekend, I don't want her to crash before then. I'll wait until Sunday night, then she'll at least have her studies and stuff, and her friends to distract her from it come Monday morning."

"Sounds like a good idea." My heart squeezed a little for the anguish that Janelle was headed for, but this was the way of college life.

Ben stared over at me. "Sorry to dump all my stuff on you. Pretty selfish. I didn't even ask about you. How are you?"

How was I? Academically I was good. My marks were high, I enjoyed my studies, and I liked my professors. Socially things were a little dim. I'd invested so much in my friendship with Teagan that when she was gone there were no girlfriends left behind that I felt close to. I barely knew Nora even now—and she'd been my roommate for nearly a year. I'd lost touch with all my other high school friends and it would be odd to suddenly text them or email them out of the blue.

Really, my only friends were Zed and Marlow, two self-professed science nerds. I snorted softly at the irony. Just last year I would've completely overlooked people like them.

My romantic feelings for Marlow aside, I felt the most comfortable in his presence. I could talk to him about anything (except matters of the heart, obviously).

I wanted to tell my brother how I really felt about Marlow. About my emotional conflict. It was hard not having anyone I could trust to talk to about it. I almost formed the words to tell him that I thought I was in love with someone who wasn't in love with me, but I saw the turmoil in his eyes with his own hard thing that he had to do and I didn't want to add my silly troubles to his real ones.

"Everything's good with me, honestly," I said, trying to sound sincere. "If there was something up, you'd be the first to know."

"Great." He stood and headed for the door. "I'll see you later."

A new kind of sadness flooded my heart when he left, knowing that by next week I wouldn't randomly see him on campus visiting his girlfriend.

I decided I didn't like change. Life could really suck.

Chapter Eight

HE SWORE CRYSTAL TO SECRECY.

"You can't tell anybody, I mean it!"

"Hey, cool your jets." She stepped closer and smiled seductively. "I love secrets."

Crystal oozed sex-appeal—there was a reason she was a media star. He couldn't believe he was alone with her in his shed. She ran a fingernail along his arm. "I need you to understand how important this is."

"I understand, Fringe. I think it's exciting. And sexy. I think you're sexy."

His knees literally gave out. Thankfully, the sofa was nearby. Crystal acted as if she didn't notice how he had melted in her presence. She curled up beside him. Not touching but really, really close.

"How many people know, besides me?"

His body tensed and his heart rate spiked at the

warmth of her breath against his neck. His mouth grew dry and he could barely spit out his response. "No one."

She squealed softly, her eyes bright. Obviously Crystal loved feeling special, and this was no different. He just wasn't so sure he could trust her. He stared into her beautiful blue eyes. He wanted to trust her. He really wanted to.

"Do you have a boyfriend?" He couldn't believe he asked her that. The question had bounced noisily around in his head like a trapped fly, but he hadn't meant to say it out loud.

"No, Fringe. I'm conveniently single."

He noticed she didn't bother to ask him if he had a girlfriend. Did she think it unlikely or did she just not care?

"Why did you call me Fringe?"

"Because when I first saw you, your hair was longer, in your eyes. What's your real name?"

He told her and she tried it out. "I like Fringe better. You don't mind?"

The way she pressed her body against his, she could call him any damn thing she wanted.

They fell into a rapid-fire fairy tale romance where the beautiful princess kissed the ugly frog. Except that Crystal had a way to make him feel desirable and movie star hot. Perhaps somewhere along the way he'd turned into the handsome prince after all.

He started walking taller, shoulders back, surfing a wave of confidence he'd never experienced before. A mischievous grin tugged on his lips.

His new demeanor didn't go unnoticed. The few friends he had laughed at him, asked him what the hell was wrong with him. He laughed back knowing full well if they knew what he had now—Crystal Morrisette in the flesh!—they'd crap their pants. And that one day they would be stunned when they found out.

Some of them thought he might be manufacturing his own drugs in the lab, a synthetic steroid or something. He let them believe whatever they wanted. Teased them by saying they'd find out when he won The New Scientist Innovation Award.

All the top science students were working on new things and most had registered for the contest. He didn't want anyone to know what he was really doing—he was afraid someone would steal his work, steal his ideas. What he had was brilliant. If he could just perfect it, control it, it would be worth millions. He'd be a millionaire! Crystal would be proud to be seen in public with him then.

For now he was okay to keep things quiet. Crystal insisted their affair remain secret. She said it was special and theirs only. And because she was a media celebrity, going public could ruin her mojo. All her followers wanted her to be single and available, girls and guys both. It was a business move that she stayed single in their eyes. He understood didn't he? Of course he did. But that didn't stop him from wishing he could show her off to his science pals.

He would keep quiet for now, because one day everyone would know.

They made good use of that old sofa in the shed and Crystal often stayed until the early hours of the morning. He'd suggested that she should take him up to her apartment—it would be more comfortable—*and* it would make him feel like he'd truly been invited into her life. Like they were an actual couple, and not like he was just her current boyfriend *du jour*, which was what he'd started to feel like.

When Crystal wouldn't budge, he suggested, "Maybe I should bring a bed in here, I could get one, you know, set it up for us."

"Nah, this space is too small," Crystal said. "You need room for your experiment. That's so much more important." She pressed close to him and nuzzled her nose in his neck. "I like that we have to squeeze together on this sofa. It's fun, isn't it?"

He couldn't disagree with that.

It was part of Crystal's brand to be bubbly and outgoing, always in a good mood, so when she started to get surly and quiet, he grew concerned. Was this the beginning of the end? Was she tired of him already? Over greasy take-out burgers he asked her, "Is something wrong?"

She pouted, her full bottom lip extending out and released a cute sigh. "Well, it's my work. I'm sort of losing steam. My followers are dropping off and I'm not gaining new followers as quickly as I'd like. I need to keep up momentum in order to gain advertiser interest so that I can make more money."

He was relieved to hear that her troubles were work related and had nothing to do with him. "Is there anything I can do to help?" He couldn't imagine what, because no one in her life even knew he existed. But he felt as her guy, boyfriend, hook-up—he really didn't know what he was to her—that he should offer.

She tilted her head—smile returning, good mood buoying—and said, "Actually, Fringe, there is."

Chapter Nine

MARLOW

PROFESSOR GARVIN WRAPPED up his lecture on the latest experiments in quantum theory. Was Schrödinger's Cat alive if we peeked at it through blurry lenses? Theoretical physicists believed, because of the famous "slit experiment", that atoms behaved according to probability, and the actual destination couldn't be determined until someone observed it. So what if the "observer" had bad eyes?

As usual, the professor left the question unanswered for us to draw our own conclusions and present them in a well-argued paper, due next week.

"You can hand your papers in to Mr. Finch," Prof. Garvin said, motioning to his TA who sat at a small table beside Garvin's desk. Rudy Finch had a look that Sage would call a "resting bitch face."

"Don't forget today is the last day to register for the New Scientist Innovation Award contest. The website is on the board behind me." Gavin rubbed his bald head and the skin on his forehead collapsed into a row of squiggly lines. "I'm not going to lie and say it's easy, but with the brilliant minds in this class anything is possible. You won't know if you don't try, and at the very least it will be a dry run for next year. Develop a hypothesis on your own or with a partner."

Zed snapped shut his textbook dramatically. "Dude, we need to enter."

He'd get no argument from me. "You got any ideas?"

"Cyborg tech."

I shook my head. "It's been done to death."

"Genetic manipulation for cosmetic purposes."

"Too unpopular. Would never win."

"Space toilet?"

I scoffed. "You're watching too much Big Bang Theory."

"Fine. You don't like my ideas, give me some of yours, Mr. Ideas-Squasher man."

A bottle jam formed at the door as students streamed out, and Zed and I were pushed up against Wyatt Banks and Isaac Cavanaugh.

"Are you entering?" Zed asked them.

Wyatt pivoted. "Damn right. Could be life-changing."

Isaac agreed. I had the feeling Isaac agreed with whatever Wyatt said.

"Are you pairing up?" I asked.

Wyatt snickered, "No way. I'm too greedy to share accolades with the likes of him. Are you guys?"

"Yeah," I said. Zed and I had been together so long, I often felt like we were one person. Siamese twins fused at the brain.

Proving my point, Zed said, "Two heads are better than one."

We were burped out the door and Zed saluted me before heading in the opposite direction. "We need to brainstorm later."

"I'll text you," I said. My mind was already spinning trying to generate the next great idea. Something physics-based would be best. Or not. I didn't want to limit myself. I also enjoyed the other sciences even if physics was my favorite.

I walked behind Wyatt, our crowd dispersing, when Harland Payne, coming from the right, head down, bumped into him.

"Hey dumbass!" Wyatt said, giving him a shove. "Watch where you're going."

Harland's face turned beet red, and though his mouth opened, no words came out. A couple of the girls who'd been watching giggled, and Wyatt ran a hand through his hair and smirked.

Jerk.

Harland looked mortified and I felt for him. He'd probably been homeschooled or special tutored and hadn't learned how to roll with schoolyard bullying.

Everyone dispersed, and I kept walking. All my bullying buttons were pushed and I wished I'd said something, but it all happened so fast. Anything I'd said would've only furthered Harland's embarrassment.

In the distance I caught a glimpse of Sage's dark hair blowing like a flag from underneath a baby blue wool hat, and I stopped short. Her chin was tucked in to her scarf and she had her books and laptop wrapped closely to her chest with arms thickened by her fall jacket.

Seeing her made something in my chest ding. I missed her. Our friendship had been forged in crisis, and now that life had calmed, we didn't know how to be friends. How was it possible that with so much shared history we had nothing left to talk about?

Maybe I should ask Sage to brainstorm with me? She was into languages and humanities, but above all she was a whiz at math. Who else besides Sage could grab hold of experiences and concepts that others couldn't even fathom? She was brilliant.

Yes, this was an excellent idea, and not just because it was an excuse to be friends again. I took a step toward her. In my mind I rehearsed my opening lines. *"Hey Sage, how's it going? Have you heard about the New Scientist Innovation Award contest? Would you like to help me brainstorm ideas? Maybe we can get a coffee?"*

I picked up my pace, but before I could reach her she was intercepted by another student, a guy I didn't know. She seemed genuinely happy to see him and my heart dropped. Shouldn't surprise me. Sage was a looker, and she was smart and popular. Of course the guys would be after her. I mean what was new about that?

I made a quick sideways crab-step behind a tree before Sage could see me.

I was an idiot. Whatever Sage and I had was over. She's moved on. I moved on.

I've moved on.

As if to prove it to myself, I dug my phone out of my pocket and with cold dry fingers sent a text to Dakota.

Chapter Ten

WHEN CRYSTAL TOLD him what she wanted him to do to help her boost her ratings, he was stunned.

"No," he said unequivocally. "That's not a good idea."

She stroked his jaw in the way that caused his blood to vacate his head and head south. "Imagine what this could do for you, Fringe. You can use my platform to present your invention, your experiment, *your discovery* to the world. Do you know how many people follow me on Instagram?"

He did know, actually. Five million and counting. He watched Crystal's Instagram account obsessively. To the point that it got in the way of his studies and his work here in the lab. He was thankful for the shower stall in the bathroom in the shed and the endless supply of cold water.

He shifted from his spot on the couch, knowing he had to put some distance between them. "I'm not ready."

Crystal was undaunted. "Why not? I've seen you experiment with it. It works!"

He jumped to his feet, stepping far enough away that Crystal couldn't reach out and touch him. "I'm not ready because I don't know what the long-term effects are." He paced like a trapped animal. "I don't even know what the short-term effects are. I've only studied my own vital signs and...."

Crystal interrupted. "Fringe, relax." Like a leopard she padded languidly toward him. The space was crowded with his equipment, leaving him little room to escape her mesmerizing gaze. She stood in front of him, pawing his biceps, and purred into his ear. "You're fine, aren't you? Nothing bad is going to happen to me." She nuzzled her nose to his neck, a move she knew drove him crazy, and whispered, "Let me be your guinea pig." She ran her fingernail along the waist of his jeans against his hot skin. "*Please.*"

He was helpless, paralyzed, like a weak-minded insect caught in a cunning spider's web. He could never deny her anything she asked for.

He gulped. "You really want me to test it on you?"

Her tongue grazed his ear. "Yes." She moved him

to the sofa. It only took the tiniest push for him to collapse on the cushions, and she straddled him. "You won't be sorry, Fringe. I promise you."

At that moment and time, he believed her. He believed her with all his heart.

Chapter Eleven

MARLOW

I DUCKED into The Literary Café by the library to grab a quick coffee, something to boost my energy and to hold off the cold that was seeping into my bones. I was immediately invigorated by the smell of fresh ground beans and warm cinnamon buns, and didn't even notice Sage when I first passed through the door. She stood at the end of the line, and I studied her profile as she read from her phone. Her hair hung over her shoulder in dark waves, and she reached up to push it behind her ear, a move I'd witnessed many times. She wore a black fall jacket and festive orange-rimmed glasses, which I knew to be a prescription-free fashion accessory as she had perfectly good eyesight. She tapped her phone and dropped it into her bag, letting out a soft sigh.

"Hey, Sage," I said as I stepped in behind her.

Sage looked startled to see me. "Oh, hi, Marlow." She blinked slowly as if searching for something witty to say, but settled for the usual, "How's it going?"

"Good. How's it with you?"

"Good."

It felt like we were both searching for what to say next. I wasn't sure how our friendship had unraveled to this point. It didn't help that we hardly saw each other. We shared one class, but didn't hang out.

Like Sage, I also wore glasses I didn't need, an emotional social shield, and a ploy Sage and I had in common. I pushed them high onto the bridge of my nose, a nervous tick, and one that Sage was aware of. So now she knew I was nervous. Great.

The line moved and we shuffled closer to the counter. Sage would be the next to order. If I was going to ask her to help with brainstorming, I had to do it now. Strictly an academic, friend to friend invitation.

"Have you heard of The New Scientist Innovation Award contest?"

Sage nodded and seemed to relax at the benign subject matter. "Yeah I have. Are you entering?" She blushed and waved her hand in front of her face. "Of course you're entering!"

"Yeah, Zed and I are going to go in together, but

you know, we're hitting a wall when it comes to,"—I finger quoted—"the great idea."

"I can see how that could be tough."

See, we were just making friendly conversation. Nothing more than that. Normal friendly chatter.

"Would you like to grab a coffee sometime?" It came out like a sneeze. I almost snagged a napkin to wipe my verbal spittle off her shoulder.

Her glossy pink lips fell open. "Dakota?"

Oh man. It sounded like I'd asked her on a date! "No, I mean—" I rubbed the back of my neck feeling amazed at how awkward this had become in such a short time. "I mean to help us brainstorm for ideas for the science award. You know, fresh eyes and a new perspective."

Disappointment flashed over her face and it confused me. I felt like I was thirteen years old again trying to figure out the mystery of the opposite sex.

Sage moved to the front of the line and placed her order—coffee with cream and sugar—then turned back to me. "Sure, Marlow. I'd be happy to help if I can."

I stood tall with relief. "Excellent. What's your schedule like? Maybe we can coordinate a time to meet." We opened our calendars and came up with a time two days from now at 3:00 p.m.

She paid for her coffee and it was my turn up.

"See you later, Mars."

"See ya."

I felt foolishly happy about my impending appointment with Sage. I almost broke out in song as I exited the coffee shop with my hot drink in hand.

Chapter Twelve

SAGE

MARLOW HAD ALREADY ORDERED coffees and had secured a table at The Literary Café when I arrived. The place was warm and inviting with soft brown walls decorated with coffee slogans, and comfortable reading chairs were tucked in the corners with short shelves stocked with used books. Take one/leave one. I draped my jacket over the back of the chair opposite Marlow. He wasn't wearing his fake glasses today and I had to keep myself from staring at his captivating green eyes. I scooted in, determined to be cool as a cucumber. Not going to say or do anything stupid. Marlow was my friend, that was all, but he was my friend.

"Thanks for the coffee," I said. "I owe you."

He waved me off. "Consider it payment for your time, and not very well paid at that."

"Where's Zed?"

Marlow hesitated, his eyes darting back and forth as they often did when he was searching for the most appropriate answer. I had the feeling he hadn't invited Zed, and wondered briefly if maybe this *was* a date, but then he stretched his leg out to retrieve his phone from his front pocket.

"He might've forgotten," Marlow said. "I'll text him."

We sipped our coffees at the same time and then said together, "So?" This was followed by nervous laughter.

Marlow said, "You go."

"How's Dakota?" Might as well take a stab at the elephant in the room right off the bat.

Marlow blinked and went to push up the lenses that weren't there and instead jabbed himself in the forehead. I pretended not to notice.

"She's good. Busy with studies like all of us. And her friends. She's not the type who needs to hang on her boyfriend's arm all the time."

His face reddened as if embarrassed to be talking about his girlfriend to me. I swallowed. "That's good."

He deftly changed the subject. "How's Ben?"

"He's good. He's planning a trip around the

world." My fingers flew to my lips. "That's not common knowledge. Please don't say anything."

"His girlfriend doesn't know, I gather."

"Not yet."

It was awkward keeping my eyes on Marlow in this close proximity and I allowed my gazed to drift around the store. "Do you remember the first time we met up here?"

Marlow's mouth curled up as he took a look around the café too. It hadn't been the first time we had met, but it had been the first time we had talked to each other while I was sober.

He pointed. "We sat at that table. You told me about the dreams you were having."

"And you pretended to not know me as well as you did."

Our eyes locked and it felt like the air in the café spiked ten degrees. I pulled on the collar of my sweater.

"And now you know me," he said.

"I guess I do." I wanted to reach over and take his hand. Squeeze it. Remind him that we were good together, that we'd be good together, but I didn't. If he and Dakota broke up, it wouldn't be because of me.

The universe seemed to read my mind because just at that moment Dakota appeared out of nowhere. "Marlow?"

Apparently she wasn't aware of our brainstorming session. Marlow's eyes widened and his Adam's apple bobbed. "Dakota, hey."

"What's going on?"

"Sage and I are brainstorming."

I quickly pulled out my laptop and opened it up. "I'm just trying to help Marlow and Zed come up with ideas for the New Scientist Award contest."

Dakota folded her arms across her chest. With her petite stature and pink pixie cut hair, she reminded me of an angry Tinkerbell. I actually checked to see if she was tapping a pointy-shoed foot. She narrowed her gaze on Marlow. "I would've brainstormed with you had you asked."

"Yeah, I know, just I didn't think..."

"You don't think I'm smart enough?"

"No that's not it. Just Zed..."

"Zed doesn't think I'm smart enough? Where is he anyway?"

"He's on his way here, just running late. You know Zed."

Fortune was on Marlow's side because right at that moment Zed blew in with a gust of wind. "Hey guys!"

Dakota had to turn away from our table to see him, and Marlow used that moment to frantically wave him over. Zed's gaze darted to me and back to Dakota, understanding flashing across his face.

"So sorry I'm late. Hey Dakota, are you joining us?"

"Apparently Marlow doesn't think I'm smart enough."

Marlow protested. "That's not true. Here." He pulled out the chair next to him. "Have a seat. I honestly didn't think you'd be interested."

Dakota huffed. "It's fine. I'm here with Payton." She motioned to a blond who was eyeing the goodies in the display. Then she bent down and gave Marlow a deep and long lasting kiss. Zed stared, but had the decency to look embarrassed.

Dakota was sending me a message, loud and clear. *Back off my guy.*

Message received. I turned to Zed and forced myself not to look back at Dakota as she wiggled away. "Should we get started?" I tried to shake this whole uncomfortable and embarrassing situation off. "What ideas have you come up with so far?"

"I think we need to ask a few questions first," Zed said. "What kinds of technology will improve the human condition? These are the kinds of things that win awards."

"How about focusing on health and improving the body?" I said.

Marlow finally lifted his gaze from his lap and joined in. "Those are two different things. The first—

restoring health—moves from a deficit to normalcy. The second moves from normalcy to a 'superhuman' status."

"Cyborg tech is always popular," Zed said.

"We've talked about this already," Marlow said. "It's been done to death."

"Yeah, but, we could develop a theory on how to effectively graft a mechanical limb to organic material. Without the seam."

"Like the terminator?" Marlow said. "We don't have the resources for that."

"I know. I meant providing a theory."

I added, "A demonstrable experiment would be more appealing to judges, I would think."

Zed shrugged. "Maybe, maybe not."

"The award will likely go to something that improves the quality of human life somehow," I said. "What about blood? Blood is life. If we can improve the blood, that would turn the judges' head." I noticed how I'd switched pronouns from "you" to "we". Zed and Marlow didn't seem to care, and I was starting to feel personally invested.

"There are already ways to increase athletic performance by increasing red blood cell count," Marlow said.

"But what about the constant shortage of blood?" I thought about the up-coming blood drive being promoted on campus. "What if you could create a synthetic version?"

Marlow and Zed both perked up at that. Marlow leaned in. "Then there would never be a shortage of blood or the needed type. It would be a lifesaving invention."

"Except if it's used on healthy people to make them stronger and more fit than normal," Zed said. "It would be easy to increase the oxygen levels, which would give athletes who were transfused with it an advantage."

"Like a steroid," I said. "Synthetic blood would have to be regulated. But just because there's an opportunity for abuse—and there always is, isn't there?—it's not a reason to not make the advancement."

"We could only provide a hypothesis," Marlow said, "and I'm sure that's already been done."

Zed finger-combed his beard. "We could design a small pressurized metal cylinder for storing synthetic blood, once it's in production, with a valve that allows gases to be introduced into it to alter it further to improve its quality."

"I like it," Marlow said with a grin. "Let's do it."

"Top secret," Zed said. "You can't tell anyone." He shot Marlow a meaningful look. "Not even significant others."

Zed placed his fist over the center of the table and

Marlow rested his on top. He looked at me and nodded. I smiled as I placed my fist on the pile.

Zed and Marlow chanted, "Boom!" and I burst out laughing, feeling truly happy for the first time in weeks.

Chapter Thirteen

MARLOW

ZED and I have been best buds since we started school back in kindergarten. I didn't have a brother so I always looked at him as sort of my pseudo-brother. He had two younger brothers so I didn't really know what he got out of his relationship with me, except that we were both nerds with no social skills and he needed me for moral support. It was true that like-species congregated together. Zed and I were never part of the popular crowd. We never had the girls. We never got invited to parties. But we always had each other.

That meant we shared a lot of things, including our prized possessions. When I got a new Nintendo, I shared it with Zed, mainly because I had no one else to play it with. We shared our DVDs, our games, our music, our notes from school. We shared our scientific ideas and philosophies and dreams. Not that we agreed on everything, but we always could engage in a friendly debate that would eat up several hours of a boring summer afternoon.

But a person had limits. For example, girlfriends. I had a girlfriend and he didn't, yet somehow he was always with me and my girlfriend. Somehow it happened that we ended up going from a duo, Zed and me, to a trio, Zed, me and Dakota. I dropped hints that maybe Dakota and I would like to be alone some of the time, but he didn't seem to get the picture. And worse yet, Dakota didn't seem to mind his company. That bothered me in a very deep, primal level, stirring up feelings I wasn't proud of.

At the moment we sat on the couch in the guys lounge, Dakota in the middle, playing *Zed's Revenge*— a game Zed had developed, while simultaneously discussing the bush party that all the sophomores were talking about.

"It's going to be so much fun!" Dakota said just as she blew up my avatar.

"Agh," I moaned.

Zed and Dakota high-fived and laughed.

"You guys are picking on me!"

"Oh, don't be a party pooper," Zed said.

I reloaded my avatar.

"Back to the subject of parties," Dakota said, "we have to go. Everyone's going to be there."

"So?" I persisted.

"So, it'll be fun."

I thumbed my way to the next level, sneaking up on Zed's avatar. "Dakota, you know how I feel about parties."

She sighed. "Marlow you have to learn to be social some of the time. Eventually you'll have a job and you'll have to go to staff parties and people's weddings." She nudged me in the arm with her elbow and I missed my next shot.

"Help me out here, Zed," Dakota said over the gunfire noise.

Ha. She'd just made a fatal tactical error. There was one thing I knew for sure and that was that Zed and I were on the same page when it came to social events. They were pitfalls for inevitable embarrassment, rejection, and endless opportunities to be the butt of other people's jokes. I could count on him to side with me.

Then he said, "She's got a point. I mean, one of these days we do have to break out of our own little bubble and mix with the masses."

My jaw went slack and I couldn't stop myself from peeling my gaze from the screen and giving Zed a lazer-of-death stare. "Are you kidding me?" I made an executive decision and paused the game.

"Hey!" Zed and Dakota cried out in unison.

I kept my angry gaze on Zed. "You actually want to go to this bush party?" He refused to look me in the eye, instead offered up a lazy shrug.

"See, Marlow?" Dakota said with a note of victory in her voice. "Everyone wants to go to this party. Think of it as a networking opportunity. Even nerds and lose-"—she caught herself quickly—"high learners need to network and integrate with the world."

She was going to say *losers*. Did she really think of me as a loser? If that was what she thought of me why was she with me?

Dakota was sensitive enough to know that I caught her faux pas. She grabbed my hand, laced her fingers through mine and kissed my knuckles. "Marlow, you know I'm crazy about you right?"

I pushed up my glasses. "If you say so."

"I do say so. I just want to go to the party and I don't want to go without my boyfriend."

I supposed that that was reasonable. My eyes cut to Zed. He folded his arms and looked somewhat dejected. I hoped he felt like an idiot for siding with her and not standing up for me.

"Okay. Let's go party in the bush!" I lifted my hand

in a hang ten, as if I was mocking those who found parties exciting. Which I totally was.

"Glad that's settled," Zed said gruffly, and restarted the game. I refocused, but from my peripheral caught sight of Wyatt Banks entering the lounge with a girl on his arm. She had long dark hair and for a split second I thought it was Sage. My heart skipped along like a rock on the water, but calmed down when I realized it wasn't her at all. Dakota would hate it if she knew how even an "almost" sighting of Sage still effected me.

Then I wondered if Sage would be at the bush party. Of course she would. That was the kind of thing Sage did. Those were her people. I scoffed a little to myself. Wouldn't she be surprised to see me there! I admitted that seeing her would make going to that party more palatable.

My mind on Sage distracted me from the game.

"And boom!" Zed shouted. "Dude, you are out again!"

Chapter Fourteen

HE WAS DEFINITELY GOING against his better judgement. "I don't know. Maybe doing this after dark is a bad idea? We should wait."

Crystal pushed her sexy, glossy bottom lip out in her signature pout. "*Fringe*, I'm not afraid of the dark. Besides it's not even that dark out yet, and it's just a trial run."

Crystal had a point. This was a test. It was twilight, the time of day when a casual observer would believe the setting sun had tricked their eyes, should someone accidentally see her. He sighed then handed her the activation device. He'd purposely designed it to look like a common cell phone.

"Okay," he said, "I'll count to three with my fingers and when my thumb goes up, you press the button, got that?"

Her beautiful eyes glistened with excitement. "Got it," she said. His heart beat nervously before he even began to count. What if something went wrong? What if he hurt her? He was having second thoughts.

Crystal glared at him with impatience. "What's the matter?"

"I'm just not sure about this. It's one thing to experiment on myself, but I don't know what I would do if something happened to you."

She softened. "Oh Fringe, you're so sweet. But really, I'll be fine. I just know it in my gut. I have complete confidence in your brilliance. I mean, you're a genius! You've done it lots of times and you're fine, right? If anything was amiss, you'd have seen signs of it by now, wouldn't you?"

He wasn't sure how to answer that. He had been feeling extra jittery these days. Along with rising anxiety levels, he suffered moments of physical clumsiness. He wasn't sure though if these symptoms had to do with this experiment or if it was the result of social stress. It could be from too much coffee, or lack of sleep. He hadn't slept much since Crystal came into his life. That was probably it.

"All right," he said. "On my count. One, two, three." His thumb snapped up and she pushed the button. Crystal Morrisette, media starlet, girl of his heart, disappeared before his very eyes. He waited thirty seconds and flipped a switch on the teleportation console and she reappeared. In one piece. He let out a breath of relief.

Her eyes were like saucers. "Oh. My. God. That was flippin' amazing!" She stepped across the room and laid a big, wet kiss on him. "Almost better than sex!"

Their plan promised to boost Crystal's popularity and her ratings. Through the frickin' roof.

"I'm going to beat the pants off of Violet Vee," she said. "Imagine when I appear out of thin air at the bush party and then disappear before their eyes? Everyone will wonder what happened, if they took bad drugs, or if they're crazy, but they'll all know it happened because they will have all *seen* it. And everyone will be talking about me. *Everyone*. I have to make sure people have their cameras on me first. I'll just flirt until some guy starts to video. They always do."

The look in her bright blue eyes was almost crazed. She was so excited. He was excited too, and could hardly wait for Friday night. He wanted to help Crystal, wanted to make her famous. He wanted to give her anything and everything that she wanted.

Life couldn't be better. Had someone told him a few months ago that Crystal Morrisette would be his secret lover and a collaborator in his science experiment, he would've laughed in their face. And yet here he was. Soon they'd be able to come out as a real couple. Everyone would want to know how they'd accomplished this miraculous feat and she'd have to tell them all about him.

Crystal was right. She was a great platform for him to announce to the world what he had accomplished. Buzz before the contest winner was chosen could only help him. And he couldn't have chosen a more beautiful, vivacious woman to be his partner in science and in life. He really couldn't be happier. In fact he hardly could conceal his joy. The few friends he had at Detroit University weren't used to his new persona. They accused him of being on happy pills. Like he was taking drugs for depression or something. He let them believe what they wanted to. Soon they would know the truth. He would no longer be the side-kick guy, the overlooked guy. No, everyone would *know* who he was. They'd cross the room to talk to him. He fantasized about being awarded a Nobel Prize for his work with the beautiful Crystal on his arm. Life just could not be better.

Then the blimp popped.

He'd come down with some kind of bug and had

dropped into a drugstore for antihistamine. He spotted her when he left the store, waiting at the bus stop. She was hard to miss with her copper red hair piled on the top of her head in a sloppy bun, with loose tendrils cascading against her forest-green fall coat. The crystal earrings he'd given her sparkled from the glow of the streetlight. He was just about to call out to her when suddenly she wrapped her arms around the neck of the man next to her—he hadn't even registered his existence until then—and kissed him. The guy cupped her face in his hands and stroked her cheek with his thumb.

He wasn't sure why it stunned him, shocked him, as much as it did. She never claimed exclusivity. Never told him that she wouldn't see anyone else. He just hadn't imagined it. She was with him all the time. Well, except for the times he was in class, or she was out with her friends. He'd been stupid to think that when she said "friends" that she meant girlfriends.

Her betrayal devastated him. Deep down in the bitter recesses of his soul it crushed him. Worse yet, he began to doubt everything that Crystal had ever said about him. All those whispers about how she found him attractive, and sexy, and dynamic. That she liked to be with him, liked to hang out with him.

He was such an idiot. Crystal was just *using* him. He was her ticket to fame. Once she'd achieved her goal, he had no doubt that she'd toss him to the curb like a sack of garbage.

He was still the plain-faced cast-off he always had been, and now he was a fool too.

People like Crystal Morrisette just heartlessly played with people like him. They were teasers, selfish bitches. They cared for no one but themselves. Crystal was with him because she wanted something from him, even if it meant using sex to get it. Sex and sex appeal was her commodity. Why was he so surprised?

There would be no point in confronting her. Women like Crystal just lied. She'd run her fingernail up his arm, grip the back of his neck and press her body close. She'd whisper in his ear, nibble on his earlobe, thinking that she would get her way again.

But she'd underestimated him. He wasn't a pushover.

She'd have a tantrum if he suddenly pulled the plug on their plans for Friday night, and he didn't want to deal with that drama. What he needed to do was teach her a lesson. Something that would show her who's calling the shots. Then she'd crawl back to him and respect him the way he deserved to be respected.

And the best way to do that was to have the experiment not work the way she planned. He might be her doormat now, but he would have the last laugh.

Chapter Fifteen

SAGE

"I'M GETTING a ride with you right?" Nora bent over the bathroom sink, and peered in the mirror with puckered lips as she applied tangerine-colored lipstick. She made a smacking noise then looked at me, waiting for my answer.

"Yeah, it's fine," I said. "Nothing's changed."

We were both getting ready for the sophomore bush party. I dressed in layers because the evening would get colder as time went on, but it could get warm too, depending on how close you stood to the bonfire. My old self would have been so excited to go out with friends. My old self would have enjoyed the processes of getting ready to go out with friends. My old self actually had friends—plural. I stared at Nora wistfully, once again wishing it were Teagan on that side of the room instead.

I was tempted to stay back and work on my German language course—I found I had a knack for languages and had registered for French and Mandarin as well—but I knew I wouldn't hear the last of it from Nora if I bailed. Why I was succumbing to her peer pressure I didn't know.

Well, I did know. I was inherently a social person. I needed friends, or at least people around me. That fact that Nora currently qualified as my "bestie" was depressing. I let out a sigh.

I wished I were home with my mom and dad to feed me comfort food. A nice long bubble bath and a good book sounded good too.

What was wrong with me? I loved parties. I loved these kind of events. I really needed to snap out of it. I was twenty years old, for Pete's sake, not fifty. But despite my internal self talk I couldn't keep myself from letting out another sigh.

Nora sat on the edge of her bed as she laced up her new trendy fall boots. "What the hell is wrong with you? I know you've had a hard go of it lately, but really, you need to get your act together. You need to get a boyfriend, you know, get *busy*. That would get you out of this funk. Like I said before, I can set you up with one of Jake's friends."

"I'm fine!" I snapped back.

She ignored my tone, undaunted in her need to play Cupid. "You've met Isaac Cavanaugh, but he isn't the only one. I know, have you met Rob Hooper? I heard he and Maggie Epstein just broke up. Or," she winked, "Chet Wiens."

There was no shutting her off. I was exasperated by the pressure she was putting on me and in normal situations I would've said this with my inside voice, or responded with a witty remark, but instead I blurted, "I already have someone."

Nora froze mid-lace-up. Her eyes widened and sparkled as her mouth curled up into a slow grin. "This makes so much sense now. Who is it, Sage? You have to tell me!"

Oh, God, what had I done?

"Is it a professor? Is that why you've been so secretive and moody?"

"It's not a professor. And I haven't been secretive and moody."

Nora scoffed, "Yeah, right."

"Honestly, it's nothing."

"Oh, no way, lady, you're not going to get away with that. 'Fess up. You gotta tell me, because I'm going to find out some way anyhow. I'm like a hound dog when it comes to digging up dirt." She laughed.

I hoped she was joking, but her earnestness frightened me. I didn't want her digging around in my life, but I knew what she was capable of if you ended up on her black list.

"It's not a big deal, Nora. I kind of like someone, but he's not available, okay? Can we drop it now?"

Nora gave me her sympathetic puppy dog look. "Oh, Sage. Unrequited love sucks." She patted the spot beside her, coaxing me to take a seat. "I know what it's like. But believe me, the best thing you can do is to tell someone and get it off your chest. And then you can move on. Honestly, I won't tell anyone. My lips are sealed." She pantomimed the locking of her lips together.

I was so exhausted by everything that happened over the last year and all of the burdens I felt like I was carrying alone, not only about Marlow, but now with Ben leaving me too. I really needed a friend. Nora wasn't that bad, really, and she was the only one offering, so I took the spot beside her and said softly, "It's Marlow Henry."

Nora couldn't stop herself from looking shocked, and she snorted. "Really? That's the guy?"

I felt defensive. "Not all great guys are athletes, and built, and could be underwear models. You have to look beyond that sometimes. Don't be so shallow."

Nora reigned in her surprise and now offered

sympathy. "No. I get it. There's a reason why they say love is blind."

It was hard to believe that Nora didn't get how offensive she was being. But she continued on in a consoling tone. "So he's with someone? He has a girlfriend?"

I nodded.

"That's why you want him. It's always the ones you can't have that you want the most."

I stood up, feeling frustrated. It had been a mistake to tell her. "Yeah, I guess you're right. I'm just being stupid. Just forget I said anything."

"Why don't you go after him?" Nora said. "I'm sure his girlfriend has nothing on you. Just steal him away."

She said it like it was the easiest thing in the world. Just snap your fingers and you've moved the heart of a guy from his current flame to you. But I knew Marlow, and he wasn't like that. He was loyal to a fault.

I wasn't like that either. I wasn't the type of girl who would purposely try to break up a good relationship to get the guy.

Nora looked at me with expectation.

"No," I said. "That's not my thing."

"Apparently you don't want Marlow Henry that badly." She strapped a sizeable purse over her shoulder. "My offer to set you up with Rob Hooper still stands."

"Thanks. I'll think about it."

My phone buzzed and I frowned.

"Who's that?" Nora probed. She really was nosy.

"It's Wyatt."

"What? Why is he texting you?"

"He's asking if I'll be at the party."

"Why?"

"I don't know."

"What a bastard. He's such a player. I mean, he's got a girlfriend!"

I squinted at her. "You just told me to steal Marlow from his girlfriend. What's the difference?"

Nora blinked and I wasn't sure she even comprehended her double standard. She stared at her reflection, again, in the mirror above her dresser. "Are you ready to go?"

"Yeah." Internally I added, *Let's get this over with.* I grabbed my black winter coat and put it on.

"So, are you going to text him back?" Nora said as we made our way outside.

"No."

"Why not?"

"Because he has a *girlfriend.*"

"How do you know? Maybe they broke up."

"Then it must've happened in the last five minutes."

"Damn, Sage. You're your own worst enemy."

I wasn't interested in Wyatt Banks. He reminded me of my old boyfriend Tristan, the kind of guy who, once he got it in his head that he wanted something, didn't give up until he got it. What I hadn't told Nora was that this wasn't the first time Wyatt had texted me. Not by a long shot. I was beginning to feel stalked. I should've just said yes to him the first time, then maybe he'd have tired of me already. These kind of guys just liked the hunt, but I wasn't going to get sucked into a relationship with another Tristan.

Chapter Sixteen

MARLOW

MY EYES KEPT DARTING to the other side of the bonfire, a monstrous, crackling stack of logs, to where Sage stood alone staring blankly into the flames. Once, she glanced up, catching me watching her. She mimicked surprise at seeing me at this party, like I knew she would, and gave me a thumbs up. I saluted. For an instant her lips pulled up softly and then dropped back into the solemn expression she'd been wearing all night.

I worried about her. She'd changed since our escapade in the summer. I guess we both had.

"Hey!" Dakota poked me in the ribs, and guilt flushed through me. Even though I constantly reassured her that Sage and I were just friends, Dakota was definitely threatened by our relationship, and catching me staring at Sage didn't help matters.

Truth was, she probably did have something to worry about.

"What?" I said, playing dumb.

She pointed to herself. "Girlfriend. Right here."

"I know, Dakota. I'm all yours."

I wrapped my arm around her thin shoulders and pulled her close. Her hair smelled like smoke, which happened to be blowing in our direction. I pulled her out of its path to cleaner air.

She wrapped her arms around my waist and pressed her cheek into my chest. "Am I?"

"Yes," I said, even as I stared over her head across the flames where Sage had once stood. Where'd she go? I glanced around, but couldn't see her. Gray clouds hid the stars in the night sky, and the air had chilled with the briskness that comes to the Midwest in October. Dakota and I pressed closer to the flames for warmth.

We were surrounded by a lot of familiar faces: Zed, our quirky dorm mates Steve and Paul, Sage's friends Jake and Nora, and even her brother Ben, who was here with his soon-to-be-ex sophomore girlfriend Janelle. Music blared from someone's stereo. Ben managed the drinks station and lectured all of us about the dangers of drinking and driving and to make sure we had designated someone to get us back safely. The sophomores remembered him from his athletic popularity from the previous year and his words carried a lot of weight. Janelle's friends hovered around her, clearly enamored by her boyfriend, and Janelle beamed with pride. Poor girl.

I finally spotted Sage again and scowled. She was talking to that jockjerk Wyatt Banks. I hadn't even known they knew each other. I gained some gratification from the fact that she looked put off. By her body language I could tell that she wasn't flirting: her arms were folded, and her hip jutted out. Then she turned on her heel and disappeared into the darkness. I couldn't help but wonder where she was going in a huff all alone. I wanted to run after her, but I felt the weight of Dakota on my arm. She was laughing at something that Zed had said that I had completely missed.

"Is that not right?" Zed said.

Dakota giggled again, "Uh, totally."

An engine started in the parking area and yellow headlights pierced the darkness. I knew the vehicle. It was Sage's new truck. Narrow beams of amber lights flashed down the road as she kicked up dirt, fish-tailing.

Had she had too much to drink? I didn't remember seeing her with a cup in hand. Or was she just really angry at something Wyatt said? Either way I felt compelled to go after her. She wasn't my girlfriend, but she was a very important person in my life. We had a connection that I didn't share with any other person on earth.

I tugged on Zed's arm and pulled him aside. "Hey, there's something wrong with Sage."

"Yeah? What?"

"She had words with Wyatt and drove away like a bat out of hell was after her."

"Wyatt?"

We both looked at where he stood beside his girl-friend, Stella. He finished his beer and opened another.

"I'm going after Sage. I just have this gut feeling something is wrong."

Zed nodded toward Dakota. "What about her?"

"I'll tell her I'm not feeling well. Can you make sure that she gets back to the dorm safely?"

Zed shrugged. "Sure, man, whatever. It's your funeral."

Dakota narrowed her eyes suspiciously when I told her that something I'd eaten earlier wasn't sitting right with me. She raised an eyebrow and pursed her lips. I didn't know if she'd seen Sage leave or not, but it was clear she wasn't happy with me.

"Seriously?"

"Yes, seriously. I think I'm going to puke.""

"How are you getting home? I drove here. Do you want me to take you back?"

"No, that's okay. I'll catch a ride with someone."

Just then I noticed Ben and Janelle leaving the party. He was my excuse, my way out. I pointed.

"I can ride with Ben. You stay, have fun with your friends."

Dakota's friend Kyra came to my rescue and tugged on her arm. She slurred, "Dakota, stay with us, 'k?"

I gave Dakota a quick kiss on the cheek rubbing my stomach to show I didn't want to give her any germs. It wasn't that I wouldn't have liked to kiss her, I would, but I had to keep my story straight. I nodded at Zed, mouthed "thanks," and then raced after Ben Farrell.

Chapter Seventeen

SAGE

DO I have some kind of jerk magnet on my head? I wanted to kick Wyatt where it hurts. Why was that the only kind of guy that seemed to find me interesting?

I climbed into Boy Toy and turned on the radio, hoping for a distraction, but it was a dumb love song and I snapped it off again. Nora was right when she said that you always want what you can't have. *The grass is always greener on the other side. You snooze you lose.* All these old adages were piercing my heart, feeling very real to me.

The guy I really wanted was already taken, and a guy I didn't want just wouldn't leave me alone. I patted the steering wheel of my truck and muttered, "It's just you and me again, Boy. You're the only one I need."

I meant it. I was off guys. It was just me and my trusty-rusty steed this year.

I sped along the dirt road. Somewhere in the back of my mind I knew I was driving too fast, the trees flanking the forest road a blur, but my emotions were blocking reasoning. Wyatt's continual advances made my skin crawl. Could you report a guy for sexual harassment if he hadn't actually touched you yet? Maybe I should tell Stella about his wandering eyes, show her his lewd texts.

I forced myself to not think of Wyatt and immediately my mind went to Marlow. I couldn't win!

I couldn't get the image of Marlow with his arm around Dakota out of my mind, or the way she clung to him like she had every right to, which she did. I envied her in so many ways—not least the fact that she was blissfully ignorant of all the wacky things that Marlow and I had experienced together. Scary and nerve-wracking and dangerous and adventurous. I didn't understand what cosmic law had kept throwing Marlow and me together in those extraordinary circumstances. Maybe it would stop now. Maybe it was over. Maybe this last year was just a fluke of sorts and now that Marlow had Dakota and I was boyfriend-free, we would live out our second year at Detroit University like normal people.

Anyway, I didn't need a guy. What I needed was an education, not a warm body.

With my mind still on the party, I was driving in auto-pilot, not paying attention to the road or my speed.

I registered the bright yellow eyes of a deer as it leaped out of the ditch ahead of me then froze in my headlights. I slammed on my brakes and my horn; the deer pivoted and darted back into the woods before I reached it.

My skin burned with a flash of fear and I started to shake, my left foot almost too weak to engage the clutch. The theater of my mind played out the image of what could've happened: deer cracking my windshield, bouncing onto the road, all bloody, broken.

I drove more carefully now, gradually increasing my speed again as my heart rate normalized.

What happened next happened so fast my mind barely had a chance to register it. A woman material-ized out of nowhere in the middle of the road, her eyes wide and mouth screaming. I wrenched the steering wheel sharply to the side, my brakes squealing on the road, but it was too late. I heard a sickening *thunk* and a crunch, then skittered into the ditch and slammed into a tree. All went black.

Chapter Eighteen

MARLOW

I HOPPED into the backseat of Ben's car, my door slamming at the same time as Janelle's who had scooted into the passenger seat. I was no romance guru obviously, but it didn't take a rocket scientist to pick up on the frosty vibes going on between them. Something had happened—perhaps Ben had let his plans slip out prematurely—and Janelle's previous over the moon happiness was squarely snuffed out.

She leaned her elbow against the door as she gazed outwards into the darkness of the parking lot. Ben snapped on his seatbelt with a heavy sigh. The air was thick, and my presence awkward. I hadn't meant to step into the middle of a lover's quarrel. Neither of them said a word, and it left me wondering if I should say anything. I figured Sage was a safe topic.

"I'm sure she's fine," I said. "She seemed upset about something that Wyatt Banks said."

Ben hit the steering wheel with the heel of his palm. "Why can't douchebags like him just stay away from my sister!"

The venom in Ben's voice made me glad that I wasn't on the antagonistic side of his acquaintance. Ben had a heavy foot and we scooted along the bumpy forest road. I wondered if I should mention that he needed new shocks. Janelle sniffled, then shuffled through her purse to retrieve a tissue.

Hitching a ride with Ben and Janelle hadn't turned out to be a great idea, but I couldn't very well disengage myself now, in the middle of a dark Michigan forest. I checked the time—only 10:00 p.m.—and shoved my phone back into my pocket. We should be on campus in twenty minutes. I'd just have to suffer through the silence and the rough ride.

Janelle pointed out the window. "What's that?"

I leaned forward to peer between their two heads, and at first didn't see anything but blackness. Ben swerved to the right and came to a stop, his headlights on a vehicle in a ditch. My stomach dropped. "That's Sage's truck!"

Ben practically jumped out of his car before it was at a full stop. I clicked out of my seatbelt and sped after him, but there was no way I could keep stride with Mr.

LEE STRAUSS

Athlete and I pulled up behind him seconds afterward, puffing like an asthmatic. Ben wrenched on the driver's door. I peeked over his shoulder still trying to catch my breath. "Sage!"

The air bag was only partially inflated. Blood smeared her face; her eyes were closed and her chin drooped to her chest. My heart stopped. "Is she...?"

Ben had his fingers to her throat checking for her pulse. "She's alive. Call 911!"

He reached for her seatbelt.

"What are you doing?"

"Getting her out of there."

"No! She might have a back injury."

"Right. I..."

"It's okay, man, just keep talking to her."

My fingers trembled, but I managed to dial 911 and the call went through.

"You've reached 911. State your emergency."

"There's been a car accident, someone's injured! Please send an ambulance."

"Where are you, sir?"

"570 B Forest Rd., North of Detroit University. Just south of the bush party spot," I added, hoping that she might know where that was.

"Emergency vehicles have been dispatched, sir. Tell me about the injured."

"Her name is Sage Farrell. She's twenty years old."

"Can you see the nature of her injuries? Is there blood?"

"Yes, yes, there's blood. But she's breathing."

She asked me my name and relationship to Sage. "She's a friend."

The whole time I was talking to the dispatcher I'd been peering around Ben, watching Sage's face. I gasped with relief when her eyes fluttered, opening halfway. I'd swear she was looking right at me. Her mouth moved slowly. "I love you."

I dry-swallowed. Had Sage actually said that she loved me?

I wanted to say, "I love you too," but Ben beat me to it. My heart dropped with embarrassment at my own idiocy. Of course she was speaking to her brother.

"Sir?" The dispatcher's voice brought me back to reality.

"She seems to be regaining consciousness. But I don't know if she can move."

"Keep her comfortable and awake as much as possible."

I shouted to Ben, "You're supposed to keep her awake. The ambulance is on its way."

Stepping back, I reeled at the seriousness of what was happening. It seemed so surreal, and something was off. Sage was on the wrong side of the road and facing the wrong way. Something must've spooked her, causing her to yank on the steering wheel and pull a one-eighty.

Janelle had been crying softly the whole time, but suddenly her sobbing turned into hysterics. "Oh my God, oh my God, oh my God!"

I rushed to her side. "What is it?"

"Over there. Look!" I followed the direction of her pointing finger and my blood swooshed to my feet. I had to bend over at the knees to keep myself from fainting. On the road not fifty feet away was a body.

Had Sage hit someone?

I roused up courage to move toward the still form. Maybe the person was still alive. I pointed the light of my phone. It was a woman, her eyes staring back at me blankly, her limbs twisted in unnatural ways. I didn't need to check for a pulse to know that she was dead.

My mind registered familiarity—I thought I might know the woman. Was she a student at DU? Had she been in one of my classes?

Then it hit me. It was the media star, the girl all the guys in the dorm were gaga about. Crystal Something.

Sirens blared in the distance and as I pivoted to return to Ben and Sage, I caught a glimpse of something on the ground. It looked like my phone—it must've fallen out of my pocket. I scooped it up, intending to call 911 again to report the body. My hands were shaking and I must have hit a wrong button. Burning white heat shot through me from the top of my head to my toes. I pinched my eyes together feeling dizzy, and let out a yelp as I was sucked into the sensation of falling. What the hell was going on with me? Was I in shock?

My eyes finally opened and I couldn't believe what I saw. I was no longer on the forest road, steps away from Sage. I was somewhere else, somewhere dark, somewhere *inside*, but I had no clue where.

Chapter Nineteen

SAGE

DARKNESS.

My ribs hurt. I tried to move but my breath caught. I groaned and felt it coming from deep within myself, a vibration in my mouth.

My eyelids were heavy, weighted: I could barely open them. There was thick moisture on my lips, the metallic flavor of blood. I was registering that I'd been in an accident but I couldn't determine where or remember what had happened. My eyes wouldn't open.

A voice. Someone calling me. "Sage!"

I struggled to open my eyes, but it was like trying to lift a hundred pounds. I fought until they were open enough to see him.

Marlow had come to help me. My heart flooded

with emotion: relief that help had arrived, and affection for my rescuer.

I wasn't dead and Marlow was here.

"I love you." The words came out raspy and dry with barely a sound, yet they pounded like ocean waves through my skull. My declaration of love. Now Marlow knew. If I died, I'd die knowing he knew the truth.

"I love you too, Sage."

His voice confused me. It didn't belong to Marlow.

"Ben?"

"I'm here, Sagey. You're going to be okay."

Outside I heard a blaring whine of sirens accompanied by flashing red and blue lights.

"The ambulance is here," Ben said. "You're going to be okay."

Suddenly there was a lot of activity.

A strange face replaced Ben's. "We're here to help you, ma'am," the man said with a firm note of authority.

There were faces—first one, then another—they were struggling to get me out, and I couldn't help but yell out in pain. They landed me on a gurney, and blackness pressed in around my eyes, and I thought I was going to pass out from the pain. A prick in my arm felt like a tickle compared to the agony spreading through my torso, but then the drugs started to kick in and the pain subsided.

Ben tried to comfort me. "You're going to be all right, Sagey."

The paramedics carried the gurney awkwardly out of the ditch. I was strapped down so only slipped a little, but enough to remind me that my body was injured. My eyes darted about searching the darkness for Marlow. I was certain I had seen his face, but I must've been confused. Marlow wasn't here. It had been Ben all along.

I was shoved into the back of the ambulance and Ben crawled in beside me. He shouted at someone before the doors closed. "... are on their way now. Just wait with the police."

"What about Marlow?" It was Janelle's voice. "I can't find him. He's just disappeared."

I hadn't been seeing things. Marlow had been here. But now he was gone. Why would he leave me?

Chapter Twenty

MARLOW

WHAT THE HELL! What just happened? I'd been in the middle of a forest road with a starless sky, filling my lungs with fresh pine-scented air, and now I stood in the darkness in a dank and stuffy place. I was outside and then I was *inside*. My mind raced for an explanation, but found none. Rows of tiny red and green lights pierced the darkness, looking like a computer console or science equipment.

"Hey," I called out. I thought I saw movement and turned to see the back of a man rushing across the room. My heart lodged in my throat. I had no weapons. If he attacked me, I had no way to defend myself. I stepped back into a fighting stance, my hands automatically forming into fists to guard my neck. It was like my psyche knew what to do, and my body knew what to do, even though my intellect had no idea.

Before the man reached me, the light flashed again and I felt a shock like I'd just stuck my fingers into a light socket.

Cold wind slapped my face. I was outside again. My mind stumbled over the impossibility of what I'd just experienced. Had it really happened or was I delirious? Maybe I'd been injured and this was all a figment of my imagination, a bad drug-induced lucid dream. Having something bad happen to Sage was my biggest fear. It made sense why I'd dream this. That had to be it.

Emergency lights flashed from police vehicles and I knew I was back at the scene of the accident. Sage's truck was still in the ditch but she was no longer in it. Janelle was still here, looking frightened and lost.

"This isn't real," I said. "Wake up!"

"I know right?" Janelle said. "This is a nightmare."

It *was* a nightmare, but was it *real*?

I touched Janelle's shoulder. She felt real.

"The ambulance took Sage to the hospital," she said. Ben is with her. Nora and Jake are coming for me. You can catch a ride. Where did you go, anyway? Did you get sick in the ditch or something?"

I didn't respond but instead took out my phone and called Zed. "Something weird is happening!"

He snorted. "With you, something weird is always happening."

"No I'm serious. It's Sage. She was in an accident, about five miles from the party. She's hurt bad. I need a ride to the hospital."

"Oh man, okay. I came with Dakota, remember. I'll get her. We'll be right there."

I waited to wake up. But when Zed and Dakota showed up and Dakota gave me a big hug, I knew it was real. I couldn't explain what happened. All I knew was I had to get to the hospital—and quick.

Chapter Twenty-One

SAGE

"WHAT'S HER BLOOD TYPE?"

"I'm not sure. B negative, I think."

"You're her brother, right?" the paramedic said. "What's your blood type?"

"We're both adopted. I'm Type A Positive. Not compatible."

Strange flashes of light. Anxious voices. Pressure on my chest. Tremendous pain I was unable to express. Something over my mouth. I wanted to open my eyes, but they were sealed. I couldn't see and I couldn't move. I was in trouble. I could hear my heart beat in my ears, but not like a normal pulse from inside my head. I heard it from a machine beside me.

"Blood pressure down!"

"Heart rate rising!"

Filled with a strange yet beautiful peace, I floated over the whole scene. I looked for the tunnel of light, wondering if this was the end of my life, and was surprised that this thought didn't worry me. I didn't see a light, only a group of people with faces hidden behind surgical masks, wearing powder blue scrubs, and working frantically over my body. The sign on the door read, "Detroit University Clinic."

"Get a bag of B Negative."

"No B Negative."

"Then O Negative, dammit!"

The heart monitor began humming.

"Quick, we need that blood now!"

"We don't have any O Negative, either!" The nurse's voice was pitched high with stress. "Wednesday's Interstate accident depleted our supply. Backup shipment arrives in the morning."

The lead surgeon grew incredulous. "None at all?"

"We're a small underfunded hospital clinic," the nurse said tersely. "You know that. Our supplies are always low."

I wondered at the irony. Synthetic blood could be used in situations like this one. Was I going to die because I missed its development?

"I can donate."

I gasped at the sight of Marlow entering the room. How he found me, I could only guess, but I was so happy to see him.

"You're not allowed in here!"

Marlow's eyes darted to my body and back to the aggressive nurse. "I'm O Negative. I'm universal."

"We don't have time to test you for HIV."

"I'm healthy!" Marlow said. "I'm still a virgin."

A moment of silence fell in the room as everyone considered how that could be true in this day and age.

The surgeon sighed. "This is really unorthodox."

"Would you rather watch her die?"

A nurse raced toward the door shouting, "I'll get the paperwork," while another one ushered Marlow into a chair, close beside my body, and prepped his arm.

Marlow reached for my hand and I *felt* it. From my

position hovering over the room I stared at my palm and wondered at the sensation. I could feel the weight and warmth of Marlow's hand. A bag connected to a line running from Marlow's arm filled with his blood. When it was half-full, they switched it to my IV stand and pumped it into me. Marlow was hooked up to a second bag.

Suddenly my perspective from above disappeared and I was back in my body. I couldn't see except for the light that filtered through my lids, but I felt the energy in the room. I heard Marlow's voice. "Stay with us, Sage. I'm here."

I planned to do just that.

Chapter Twenty-Two

WHAT HAD MEANT to be a lesson to Crystal had turned out horribly, horribly wrong. He had hated her, but now he grieved for her. He never meant for her to die. She was supposed to have come back to him and apologize for using him. He was going to forgive her and they were to have become a real couple. And now she was dead.

The police had come to investigate her apartment. He watched out the window, entranced, as Lambert talked with large hand gestures answering whatever questions the police were asking. He thought they might come to his door, so he was ready for them when the knock came. He took his time to answer, but not too long—he didn't want them to suspect he was hiding anything, but he didn't want them to know he'd been watching them either. He opened the door keeping his expression blank. "Is something wrong?"

"Hello, sorry to disturb you. Were you acquainted with your neighbor, Crystal Morrison?"

"Just in passing. We'd say hello and stuff."

"We're sorry to have to inform you that she has been killed in a vehicle accident."

He widened his eyes as if he was hearing the news for the first time. If the cops had a warrant to search his place, they would find traces of Crystal's blood. His heart raced at the memory of her return, not the exuberant, beautiful girl who'd left moments before, but a grotesquely twisted bloodied corpse. At first he hadn't been able to believe his eyes. It had to be a sick joke! He fell to his knees at her side, checked her wrist for a pulse, but found none. She was dead and he had killed her! Pain stabbed his heart with a tidal wave of grief and he stifled a scream.

Then the urgency of the situation kicked in. He had to get her body out of his shed, couldn't be connected to her in any way. Impulsively he sent her back to the same coordinates as before, which it now appeared, had turned out to be a smart move.

"Really? That's terrible," he said, injecting just the right amount of sadness into his voice. Not too much, or they'd guess he and Crystal had been close, and not too little or they'd flag him for his lack of empathy. "She seemed like a nice girl."

The two officers glanced at each other, "I'm sure she was. Good day, then."

He closed the door to the police and caught his breath. He didn't know what he'd been worried about. They thought her death was an accident. How could they possibly tie him to that?

But there was still one huge complication: the intruder who ported in that night. The lights had been out because he didn't want to chance Lambert stopping in, which he might have done since the rent was over-due. Because of the darkness he didn't think the inter-loper knew where he had landed. He was probably super confused; hopefully he was drunk and just thought he imagined everything.

But what if he wasn't? What if the guy had been able to make out his face? He'd had to expose his profile so he could see where he was going, in order to get to the computer and send the guy back out. He'd tried to keep his back to the intruder, but was that enough?

Chapter Twenty-Three

SAGE

EITHER HALF AWAKE or half-asleep I wasn't sure, but my mind slogged through a dense fog-like dream-state to eventual physical awareness, followed by disconcerting confusion. The room I was in wasn't my own and the accompanying sounds were strange. Humming and soft, steady beeping. The lighting was dim, yet I squinted against it as if I were under a spotlight.

"You're awake," someone said. "That's good."

The woman wore mint-green scrubs. I was in a hospital. I tried to speak, but my throat was too dry. My tongue barely wetted my chapped lips.

"I'm Debbie," she said as she held up a white Styrofoam cup filled with chips of ice. "You can suck on these." I heard the whirr of a motor and the top of my bed began to incline. I savored the cool ice as it melted in my mouth and eased my dry throat.

"Thank you."

I tried to sit up of my own accord and pain shot through my chest. I gasped and relaxed back into the mattress.

"What happened to me?"

"You were in an accident," Debbie said kindly. "Your ribs are bruised, and you cut your head on the steering wheel which left you with a moderate concussion. You hit it hard enough to lose consciousness."

That accounted for the constant ache in my head. I gently fingered the wound. "I gather my airbag malfunction."

"It happens. You lost a lot of blood, and had us worried for a while." She smiled. "But you'll be okay."

"What caused the blood loss?"

Her eyes went to my right wrist that was wrapped tightly in gauze. "It was kind of a freak injury. A piece of glass from the broken windshield had lodged into the underside of your wrist. It was dark and you were dressed in black, so your brother didn't notice."

"You mean I was bleeding out?"

"Yes. It's a good thing the ambulance got there when they did."

I searched my memory banks, desperate to recall

the incident. Then slowly, the scene came to me. It was dark and I was driving too fast. I was angry. Then so quickly, the woman and the sickening thud as I hit her, the truck spinning and crunching into the tree.

My heart raced at the horror of it. "Did I kill her? Did I *kill* her?"

The heart monitor started beeping erratically. Debbie frowned then adjusted something on my IV. "It's best if you just rest for now."

"No! I need to know. Please."

Everything went fuzzy, and my head sunk back on my pillow as I slipped into a drug induced sleep.

I slept a lot over the next week, until eventually I was awake more than I slept. Ben and my parents visited me often.

At present it was my mother at my side. Her soft, creamy brown hand held mine as she drank me in with soft-brown eyes that showed the strain she was under. "You're looking better."

"Thanks, Mom. I feel a bit better."

She smiled her bright-white toothy smile. She wore a peasant blouse, and a colorful head band held her mid-length afro off her face. Ample hips filled her stretchy jeans. I always thought she was so pretty.

"I'm fine, Mom. I'm not going to die. You should go back to work."

Mom was a teacher, the good kind who loved her job and cared for her students. More than one graduate from her school had thanked her in their farewell speech for the impression she made on their lives.

"Are you sure? I could call Ben."

"It's fine. The nurses here are fully capable. If anything strange happens, they'll call you right away."

"Okay. If you're sure."

"I'm sure."

She pressed her generous lips to my forehead. "Get well, my dear."

I fell into a light sleep, in large part because I didn't have anything else to do. My brain wasn't clear enough to focus on school or even read a book and I knew rest would help me recover, so I didn't fight it. Some time later nurse Debbie nudged my arm. "Sage? Wake up. There is someone here to see you."

She nudged me again and I moaned. I heard her voice. "Maybe you can come back?"

Someone to see me? I wondered fleetingly if it was Marlow, and I didn't want him to be turned away. I'd wondered why he hadn't come before now, but then, the doctors had said family only in the beginning. I struggled through dry lips, "It's okay. Let him in."

Debbie showed me the remote I could use to raise and lower my bed. The whirring noise cut in again as it slowly raised me to a higher incline.

Debbie handed me a Styrofoam cup of water and I sipped noisily through the straw. That was when I noticed it wasn't Marlow waiting in the doorway, but a middle-aged man in an ill-fitting suit with a thick mustache and thin hair.

"Sage Farrell?"

I nodded.

"I'm Detective Landsky. Can I ask you a few questions about what happened on Friday night?"

"Okay," I said cautiously.

He tucked on his belt buckle and rolled up on his toes "Do you know what happened Friday night?"

"I think so."

"So, you understand you hit a pedestrian?"

"Yes. But I swear, she came out of nowhere. My headlights were shining on open dirt road. And then *bam*, there she was."

Detective Landsky ignored my plea of innocence. "Is it true that minutes before you left an out-of-doors party where alcohol had been served?"

"Yes, but I didn't have anything to drink."

"How fast were you driving, Ms. Farrell?"

"I don't recall."

I was beginning to feel like I should have a lawyer present. "Detective Landsky, I know a girl died, but it was an accident." I felt tears burn at the back of my eyes. Hearing myself say it just made it feel more real. *A girl died.*

He smoothed out his giant mustache. "Did you know Crystal Morrisette personally?"

"Crystal Morrisette? That's who I hit?"

The chick all the guys were raving about?

"Did you know her?"

"Not personally. She has... had a popular Instagram account. A lot of people knew who she was."

The lump in my throat swelled. The fact that the dead girl now had a name and I could picture her face just made the nightmare more dreadful.

Detective Landsky's eyes flitted around the hospital room landing on the monitoring equipment and then back to me.

"I understand you are to be released soon."

"The doctors are happy with my recovery. Nothing a few slow days and a pain killer can't cure."

"I'm glad to hear it. Up and running before you know it."

I read the subtext: *unlike the other girl.*

"I was lucky."

Detective Landsky grabbed his buckle and rolled on his toes again. "Well, good." He turned to leave and then, as an after thought, said, "I'll need to speak with you again when you're feeling better."

Chapter Twenty-Four

MARLOW

THE DETROIT UNIVERSITY LIBRARY elicited the same sense of quiet and awe as a museum. High ceilings, low hanging lights and dark paneled walls cluttered with framed paintings of prominent American leaders—the founding fathers of the university up to the present university president; roll call of all the Detroit city mayors; and of course, every single American president.

At one time, I imagined, the library had been quite upscale, built with the best wood and decorated with the finest finishings that suited the prestige of our early academics. Now the emerald green carpet was worn and cobwebs had found permanent homes in the out-of-reach decorative moldings and window ledges. The heavy wood tables and chairs were scratched and scuffed, the dark stain uneven where elbows and palms had worn away at the surfaces over the years.

It was hard to focus on studies, after what had happened to Sage. Quite honestly, I didn't know how I managed to pass my biology lab. She was well enough to text me now and last I'd heard from her, she was going to be released from the hospital soon.

I spotted Dakota—her pink hair was hard to miss— and Zed was there too, sitting across from her.

Of course he was.

They were talking quietly over the table in what appeared to be an intense conversation. So much so that they didn't even notice me approach. There was something about them that made me stop short.

"It's just so frustrating," Dakota said. "It's like I don't exist for him, not really. Only when it suits him."

"That's not true," Zed said. "He just has a lot going on right now."

"Like Sage." She snorted. "There's always something going on with him that has to do with Sage. But it's not like I can be angry with him this time. It's not like Sage got into this accident on purpose."

Zed reached over the table and clasped her hand. "Marlow—"

I cleared my throat and continued toward them,

taking a seat beside Dakota. Zed drew his hand back and slid it out of sight under the table. I pulled Dakota close and kissed her. "Hello. Sorry I'm late."

She smiled weakly. "It's okay."

I glared at Zed, channeling Charles Xavier's telepathy powers, letting him know how much I didn't like that he'd taken Dakota's hand. "Marlow what?"

He decided to play dumb. "Huh?"

"I heard you mention my name."

"Oh, I was just about to say you'd be here any minute, and look, I was right."

Liar, liar, pants on fire.

Dakota opened her laptop and without looking me in the eye asked, "Have you heard anything about Sage? How is she?"

"The doctors are happy with how her recovery is going. She's going to get out of the hospital soon."

"That's good."

"Yeah, it is."

We managed to segue out of that awkward moment to our actual studies and Zed even dropped a joke or two to keep things light. Things started to feel normal for a few seconds—until I sensed a change in the energy and atmosphere of the room. It was like, for a split second, everyone had stopped breathing all at the same time.

I turned to see what could be the cause of this

phenomenon and gaped when I saw Sage walking across the library to an empty table. She kept her head down, a curtain of soft curls hiding her eyes as she took a seat and opened her laptop.

What's she doing here?

Killer!

Life for a life!

If I could hear the murmurings then she could too, but she kept on working like she was the only person in the room.

My heart stammered as I watched her.

Dakota elbowed me in the ribs. "Staring is rude."

"I wasn't staring."

Zed scoffed. Loudly. "Dude."

"Fine. I was just surprised to see her here. I thought she was still in the hospital."

I righted myself, which put my back toward Sage. Every cell in my body was jumping. I wanted to go talk to her, but didn't know how I could extract myself without hurting Dakota.

"Just go."

"What?"

"Just go talk to her," Dakota said.

"Are you sure?"

"If that's what it takes to calm you down. You're a jumble of nerves."

"I'll only be a couple minutes. Just to see how she is, then I'll come right back."

Dakota sighed. "Do what you have to do."

I kissed her cheek. "I'll be right back."

Chapter Twenty-Five

SAGE

OKAY, maybe this wasn't a good idea.

It'd been two weeks since the accident, but it felt like two months. I loved my parents and my brother, but they were smothering me. Always checking in, always bringing food, always asking how I was feeling. Ben was the worst. I worried about him—on the same night he'd broke up with his girlfriend, he watched his sister almost die. He looked like a worn-out old man.

The thought of coming back to DU was a relief—a break for all of us—but now I wondered if I'd made a mistake. I went from being a patient to a pariah. From not having enough personal space to having an extra wide and unnatural berth.

The library was quiet except for when it was not— like now. I'd have to be deaf not to hear what people were saying about me. I worked to keep my expression neutral and pretended to be engrossed in my studies.

I looked up once and caught Stella glaring at me from one table down. I hadn't noticed her when I came in. She mouthed, *murderer*, and I quickly looked away.

Maybe I should just go back to my dorm room. If Nora was still there with Jake, I'd ask them to leave. Nora had gotten used to me being gone, and now she acted like she owned the place and that I was intruding on her privacy. Too bad. It was my room too.

I'd just closed my laptop when someone took the chair beside me.

"Marlow?" I whispered. "Hi!" It was so good to see a friendly face. His smile was sincere and when he poked his forehead in search of his glasses, I almost felt joyful.

"Hi. I didn't know you were out of the hospital."

"I've been bed resting at my parents place the last few days, but it was getting too claustrophobic. I thought I might as well come back. No sense getting further behind if I don't have to."

"And you're feeling okay?"

"My ribs hurt a little but not nearly as bad as they did. My headache's gone but," I pointed to my forehead, "this will leave a scar." I lifted my right arm. "Stitches in my wrist are coming along too." I forced a smile. "I'll be good as new in no time."

"Good."

"Thank you for donating blood. You saved my life."

"It was nothing."

"Mars, your blood is coursing through my veins."

His eyes locked with mine. The moment was supercharged and neither of us had a follow-up to my comment. We'd inched closer in order to keep our voices low, and his nearness made me feel vulnerable.

"I saw it all," I said.

"Saw what all?"

"The doctors and nurses freaking out. You giving blood."

Marlow wrinkled his nose in confusion. "What do you mean? How?"

"I saw it from above."

His eyebrows jumped. "You had an out-of-body experience?"

"Yes."

"Wow. Really? I didn't think you were that close to...." Marlow's face lost color and I rushed to reassure him.

"I wasn't dying. I don't think. At any rate, I'm here now."

Marlow leaned back to take in what I'd just told him. I let my gaze drift beyond him and that's when I saw Dakota and Zed staring. Neither of them looked too happy. I smiled and finger waved. Only Zed waved back.

Marlow witnessed the transaction. "I should get back to them. You want to join us?"

Before I could come up with a polite way to say no, my phone buzzed. I checked the caller and frowned. "Oh, oh."

"Who is it?" Marlow asked.

"Detroit police."

Life was full of new experiences. For instance, I now knew how cool and damp the ink pad was when you got fingerprinted, and how uncomfortable the bench in a jail cell at the police station was.

Apparently there was paperwork involved in making my arrest official. *Manslaughter*. Not only was I responsible for someone's death, I'd have a criminal record. My stomach churned with remorse and despair. My life was ruined.

Detective Landsky had called me into the station to formally charge me. He spoke to me through the bars. "Ms. Farrell? You have the right to a phone call."

My first thought went to Marlow. He was the one I wanted with me, the one who could possibly make sense of what has happened here, but it would be odd to call him when Ben was available. Ben would do something; find me a good lawyer. And then there were my parents. They should hear this news from me before it got to them some other way.

"Ms. Farrell?" The detective prodded.

I stared up at him and answered, "I want to call Marlow Henry."

I almost burst into tears again when Marlow was escorted into my cell. He was such a welcoming, comforting sight. I sniffled into the tissues that the officer had handed me through the bars. Once I'd talked to Marlow on the phone and knew he was on his way, my defenses collapsed. A torrent of tears let lose and I needed more tissues than the officer had given me. There was an awkward moment where we exchanged his clean ones for my wet ones.

"I'm sorry," I said to Marlow. "I'm just really emotional right now."

Marlow lowered himself onto the bench beside me. "I can imagine," he said. "You've been through a lot."

I wished I could've looked into a mirror before he arrived. I cringed a little knowing my eyes were puffy and my nose an unflattering red. I held my fingers to my face in a vain effort to camouflage it.

Marlow's knees jiggled against the bench. His eyes moved from my face to the space we found ourselves alone in.

"Nice digs."

"Yeah, they decided I deserved my own place."

"Do you know what's going to happen next?" Marlow asked.

"I'm not sure. I'm going to need a lawyer, but I don't know how I'm going to pay for that. My parents don't make that much money."

"They'll assign someone to you."

"I know." I just doubted how good a state-appointed lawyer would be, especially in this unique situation.

His green eyes filled with sympathy. "Sage, this wasn't your fault."

"I hit a person and she died, Marlow. She's dead because of me."

Marlow whispered, "That's not true."

"What do you mean? How can it not be true?"

"This is going to sound crazy, but hear me out. It wasn't your fault."

"How could it not be my fault?"

"Because she'd been teleported and she just

happened to land in front of your car. Call it bad timing."

I didn't know what I expected him to say, but it wasn't that. "Teleported?"

"Look..." He shuffled closer and I got the feeling that my already tragic situation was going to get a lot more tragic.

"While I waited for the ambulance to arrive for you, I picked up what I thought was a phone on the road by Crystal Morrisette's body." He grimaced when he said *body*. "I thought mine had fallen out of my pocket somehow, but it wasn't mine. I touched it, and suddenly I was somewhere else."

"Somewhere else?"

"Yes."

"Where were you?"

"I don't know. In someone's lab. It was dark, but I wasn't alone. I could see a man there, but only his profile. I thought he would attack me or something, but he only typed on his computer. Then I was back in the forest."

"Are you serious?"

He nodded. "Super serious."

"Oh." That did make me feel better. If what Marlow said was true, there was no way I could've prevented this accident from happening. She literally had come out of nowhere. "How do I tell something like that to the police? Even if it's true—and I believe you," I added quickly, "it's not going to help me."

"You can't go to prison for this, Sage. We'll figure something out." He squeezed my hand. "I promise."

I loved the feel of his palm in mine and I squeezed back. His concern for me just made my heart long for him even more. I never felt alone when I was with him.

We sat wordlessly, wondering what our next move should be, when, to our utter amazement, in walked Jack Henry.

He grinned through the bars at us like the cat who just ate the mouse. "Hello, Marlow. Hello, Sage. I understand you have a problem."

Chapter Twenty-Six

MARLOW

AT FIFTY-ONE JACK HENRY was in pretty good shape, with only a slightly noticeable belly pressing against his belt-buckle. He wore a white cotton shirt under a suit jacket along with an overcoat, and under that, stone-washed jeans. His hair had thinned over the years, but he still had most of it.

He also happened to be my father, though we'd only really gotten to know each other the previous summer, and now he lived with my mom in a middle-class Detroit suburb.

After reassuring Sage not to worry, and that he'd take care of things for her, he asked me to come with him for a drive. I didn't hesitate to slide into his light gray older-model Buick sedan, though I hated having to make an excuse to Dakota and Zed.

"Where are we going?" I asked.

"To see where the victim lived."

I wasn't sure what he hoped to find there.

"How did you know, about... everything?" I asked.

"I told you before, I work for a classified organization that monitors unusual activity."

"You're saying you have equipment that picked up the guy's teleportation signal?"

"Something like that."

The fact that he didn't even blink at the phrase "teleportation signal" was telling.

"I'd like to hear what happened from your perspective, Marlow."

I ran through my teleportation story again.

"And you didn't recognize him?" he asked

I shook my head. "I only caught a sliver of his profile. Average height, typical haircut."

"Did he see you?"

"It was dark, but he obviously knew I was there."

"Too dark to see your face?"

I could see in the dark, but it was a mutation and not something other people could do. Now Jack had me worried. Maybe this guy was like me.

"I don't know."

Jack let out a sigh.

"How much do you know about Crystal Morrisette?" I asked.

"I know she had a lot of followers on Instagram."

"Yeah, a lot of the guys at DU followed her."

Jack chuckled. "Not surprised. She was beautiful. So unfortunate she was killed. We need to find the asshole who did this."

Jack signaled and turned down an alley behind a pawn shop and a burger joint in a run-down, lower-class area of town. These weren't the kind of streets you'd want to be out alone on in the dark, especially as a woman who lived alone. I was a bit surprised that this was where Crystal Morrisette had lived.

Jack parked his car. A shed to the right looked like it was in use, if you could go by the cigarette butts that were on the ground around it. The windows were dark and there didn't appear to be anyone about. Jack zigzagged up a set of wooden steps located on the back side of the pawn shop and I followed him. He peered into the windows and I nervously glanced over my shoulders to see if anyone was watching us. This was a pretty obscure little alley with mature trees and no sight lines from neighbors to where we were standing.

Jack extracted a pair of latex gloves from his pocket, the blue kind like you see on cop shows on TV, slipped them on and tried the doorknob. It was locked. He glanced at me before removing a set of what appeared to be lock picks. I raised my eyebrows—Jack always was full of surprises. He had us inside Crystal's apartment in less than ten seconds.

"Don't touch anything, Marlow, and I mean anything."

I slipped my hands into my pockets. I didn't want to leave my DNA behind in this place and I was nervous about my shaggy head of hair. I'd never been tempted to get a buzz because it was a jocky thing to do but now it suddenly seemed like a good idea.

The late afternoon sun blazed in through the small kitchen window letting enough light into the living area that we could see without needing to flip a switch. Crystal's apartment sparkled. It seemed that Crystal had been interested in actual crystal. A crystal chandelier hung from the center of the room. There was a matching set of white shelves filled with little crystal ornaments: from stars and moons to birds, squirrels, dogs, rabbits, unicorns, turtles, mice... There was even a crystal alligator.

Jack entered Crystal's bedroom and I followed, stepping over piles of clothes and books. This whole thing made me really uncomfortable. Besides seeing all her lingerie flung about, I was nervous that we might get caught.

"We shouldn't be in here."

"You're only just coming to that conclusion?" Jack said

He fished through Crystal's dresser and her closet, unperturbed by the presence of female undergarments and private things.

"What are you looking for?"

"I'll tell you when I see it."

"And if you do find something, what exactly are you going to do with it?"

"That's up to the higher-ups."

The higher-ups. Jack was tight lipped about whom he worked for and I knew that was all I was going to get from him. He pulled out his phone and started snapping pictures. "What are you taking pictures of?"

"Anything and everything. You never know what you'll discover when you're examining a photograph later. The mind catches more when the pressure is off."

Crystal hadn't been one for tidiness. Her bed was unmade, the bathroom vanity was full of open containers of makeup, and toothpaste spotted the mirror. I decided to wait for Jack in the kitchen and keep a look-out through the window. I noticed there was a clear view of the shed across the alley. It made me curious as to what was in there. What did Crystal see when she looked out this window and the lights were on there?

"We should check out that shed across the way," I said.

Jack joined me and stared out the window too. "You're right."

We locked up Crystal's apartment, careful not to move anything out of place, and headed for the shed. I stood guard while Jack tapped on the door, then when nobody answered, worked his magic with the lock picks. He flicked the light switch and handed me a pair of gloves.

"What do you think of all this equipment?"

"Not sure."

Someone either lived here or at least hung out here. Somebody who liked computers and had access to lab equipment. Whoever it was ate often from the burger joint if you could go by the pile of trash on the counter. Not much else in the room besides an old table and a stained sofa. "Looks like someone is dismantling and on their way out," Jack said. "Doesn't it?"

"I suppose we really don't know what this space has been used for."

I examined the computer system and the lab supplies. "Some of these are stamped with 'Property of DU.'"

"A student, maybe?" Jack said.

I spotted something shiny tucked beside the sofa. I picked it up and showed it to Jack. A crystal owl. "I've seen this before," I said. "Crystal recently posted this as a new gift from a fan." I knew this because I'd creeped her Instagram feed after finding her dead.

"You think that a fan of hers lived here?" Jack asked.

"I suppose if she lived across the alley she would have encountered the person who stays here."

Jack flipped off the light switch. It had grown dark out in the meantime and we didn't want to draw attention. I blinked, my eyes not yet adjusted to the sudden darkness, and felt a sense of déjà vu. Jack stood at the door waiting for me. "Are you coming? We should get going before someone sees us."

I couldn't move, my mind racing. Jack noticed. "Are you okay, Marlow? Is something wrong?"

"I think this is the place. I think this is the place I was teleported to."

Jack stepped back into the room and locked the door, leaving the light out.

"Okay, walk me through it," he said.

"When you turned out the light, for a second I couldn't see, but I sensed my surroundings." I took a step forward and turned on the computer console. "I remember this light sequence. And the smell. I remembered it being stale and sweaty. "I think this was the place."

Chapter Twenty-Seven

THE SECURITY SYSTEM had been a smart move on his part. Not only to prevent theft of equipment and ideas, but to record any unusual phenomena. For example, the entry of a trespasser.

The fact that someone knew about him and his work caused him a great deal of stress. Not only because the interloper could steal his ideas and rob him of his rightful accolades, but he could be implicated in the death of poor Crystal.

Poor, poor Crystal.

He hated how she was no longer around to stroke his ego. He missed her curves and wished she were here right now so he could take her.

Crystal's betrayal had infuriated him, but still he didn't want her to die. He just wanted her to change.

One thing was certain. He couldn't go to prison.

Her death was just a big mistake. An accident. He hadn't meant for it to happen.

He had to protect himself now. He'd been pushed off course and now he was forced to make a correction. He had to eliminate further threats to his rights to property and ideas.

The night vision application on the security camera had caught the intruder's image. Enough details on the man's face for the face recognition software he'd linked to DU's registrant file, which he had hacked into. There was a match.

The encroacher's name was Marlow Henry.

Chapter Twenty-Eight

MARLOW

I FORCED down the bile that was surging up my throat, feeling squeamish at the sight of the feline corpse splayed open on its back, and grateful that Brandt Rheinhold, who happened to be my lab partner, had no such qualms. The science track encouraged study in all the sciences including biology, but I preferred the cerebral version of science like math and physics. My stomach never turned while studying atoms, and keeping down my lunch while processing quantum theory was always a safe bet.

My phone vibrated and Jack's name popped up on the screen.

Jack: I'm heading out to the scene of the accident. Want to join me?

My lip tugged up in a half grin. I'd lie if I said it didn't feel great to have Jack include me.

Marlow: Sure. When?

Jack: Now. I'm in lot B.

A reason to dodge picking apart cat guts. Hell yeah.

Marlow: On my way.

I whispered to Brandt as I packed my things. "Something's come up. I gotta run."

He glanced up from the notes he was taking and scowled. "You're leaving in the middle of a lab?"

"Sorry man. Can't be helped."

The professor was busy assisting a student in the front row, which gave me a perfect chance to leave without notice. Not that she'd try to stop me, but I didn't want to give her a reason to lower my grade if I could help it.

It took me five minutes to slow jog to lot B. I recognized Jack's Buick and kept my pace up until I reached the passenger door.

"Hey, Jack," I said as I caught my breath. I clicked on my seatbelt, and Jack pulled out into traffic. His car smelled of onions, which probably came from a recent burger consumption if the crap on the passenger floor was any indication. I rolled down the window a smidgen.

"So what's up? I mean, I assume the scene has already been picked over by police and forensics?"

Jack nodded. "Yup. I still want to see it up close with my own eyes."

"Yeah, me too."

Jack headed north in the direction of the bush party spot. I wondered what Jack and I would talk about for the next twenty minutes. He wasn't the type to listen to the radio. Said he needed his mind free to work out his cases. The silence between us didn't seem to bother him. I scrubbed my palms nervously. My knees jiggled like they had a mind of their own.

Jack glanced over. "You dancing to a song only you can hear?"

"Oh. No." I pointed to my ears. "No ear buds." I kind of wished I had them with me now.

Jack's mouth pursed, like he was holding in a grin.

"How's Mom?" I asked. I'd worried that he and my mother were moving too fast when Jack moved in this summer, reclaiming his spot as my mother's husband and my father. But my mom had adjusted well. I'd never seen her so happy in all my life as she was now. I, on the other hand, found it difficult to hand off my role as "man of the house," after holding the title for seventeen years. I was happy to be back to DU and leaving the long-lost lovers alone to rekindle whatever it was that needed rekindling.

"She's good." He smirked and arched a brow. "Really good."

That bile response I had in the lab resurfaced. No kid, no matter how old, wants to know about their parents' sex life.

He continued, "But she misses you. You didn't call last weekend."

"Yeah, sorry, I forgot, with all that happened this week. I'll call her."

"Good."

Jack had taken the highway that circled around the west side of the campus and signaled off onto some side street that led to the same forest road you could get to if you cut through DU.

More dead space. I pretended to be enthralled with the wall of spruce trees along the side of the road. If I lowered my window I could stretch out an arm and slap a branch.

"How'd you end up with that cute little girlfriend?"

My gaze darted to Jack. Was he asking me how Dakota and I got together, or how it was possible someone like me could snag a cute girlfriend? I was going to assume it was the former.

"We met at a coffee shop. She was in line in front of me and I asked her the time. She caught me out because it was obvious that my phone was in my front pocket. I bought her coffee and we made plans to meet up again."

"Really? Smooth move, Marlow. I'm impressed."

I grinned. "Yeah, I guess it was pretty smooth. It worked anyway. We've been together for four months.

Jack hummed.

"What?"

"Nothing. I'm just wondering where Sage fits in."

"What do you mean?"

"I'm no Cupid, but I've seen the way you look at each other."

"We're just friends."

He eyed me with suspicion. "Okay. If you say so."

We pulled up to the area of Sage's accident and Jack parked his car approximately thirty feet from where I'd found Crystal Morrisette's body. I shuddered at the memory, then hopped out before Jack could ask any more probing questions.

"What are we looking for?"

"An entry point for Crystal. I want to confirm that she really did 'appear out of thin air'. If you find anything, let me know. Look for clothing snags, personal effects, footprints, stuff like that."

"Wouldn't the police have gathered it up already?"

Jack shrugged. "They might've missed something."

My eyes searched the landscape ahead of us. Things looked way different in the light of day. I locked onto the damaged tree that Sage hit and my mind immediately pulled up the file on that night. The truck had a hardy bumper, so unbelievably, the vehicle hadn't suffered that much damage. The drivers' seat had been drenched in Sage's blood—I wondered if they'd get that cleaned—but Sage said the mechanic thought it could be ready to drive again in a week.

My emotions immediately replayed the scenario too. My heart beat against my chest as the memory of my fear for her life reverberated through my bones. The most important thing going forward for me was to keep Sage out of harm's way.

"Marlow? Are you okay?"

I snapped out of my revelry.

"Uh, yeah. I'm fine."

Jack surveyed the scene, staring carefully at the ground, stooping low to examine something. Shook his head.

He stopped at an indentation on the gravel. "Was this the spot?"

I joined him. "Yeah. This was were we found her."

"Where did you find the device?"

I looked around and frowned. "I'm not sure. It's all kind of a blur."

"Wager a guess."

"Well, I was on this side of the body because I'd

come from Sage's truck." Jack's eyes moved to the damaged tree and back to me.

"Janelle was standing about ten feet from Crystal Morrisette's head, so I was about here." I moved over a couple feet.

"How did you spot the phone in the dark?"

I scrubbed my forehead as I tried to remember the details of that night. "It flickered. First green then red. I didn't think anything of it at the time. When I picked it up it no longer flashed. It felt like my phone, same size, shape and weight. I touched it to bring up the number pad so I could call 911.

I looked up at Jack. "That was when I..."

He finished for me. "Teleported."

"Yeah, teleported. Up until it happened, I didn't even think it was possible? Did you?"

"No."

"So how did it happen?"

"That's what we're trying to figure out."

We continued our search giving up about an hour later when nothing turned up. No broken branches or clothing snags to indicate Crystal had somehow wondered onto the road from the forest. No personal effects such as lost jewelry or a scarf. Of course, if it was something that obvious, the police would already have it tagged in an evidence locker.

No deep tire marks other than from Sage's truck either.

"If I... teleported out and back in.... Maybe the same was meant to happen to Crystal, only in reverse. In and then out."

Jack worked his lips. "Except the person behind the controls didn't account for a random vehicle driving across his coordinates at the same time. Marlow, I believe we're looking for someone who has developed teleportation technology." He snorted. "Our killer is some kind of mega genius."

I huffed. Great. Just great.

"Did you find out who rented the shed?"

"Nope. Lambert took payment under the table. Said the guy didn't leave a name. The old man gave a description, but he wasn't big on noting details."

"Goes with running a pawn shop, I suppose."

Chapter Twenty-Nine

SAGE

JACK HAD MANAGED to get me released from custody on bail.

The condition of my release was that I had to remain in Detroit, either at home or at DU. I'd lost so much already—a social life for instance. And Marlow—that I didn't want to add my education to that. I bucked up and returned to my life as a student.

Actually, I hadn't lost Marlow. I just had to accept that I was a lower priority to him than he was to me. Fine. But neither of us could deny our connection. Marlow's teleportation experiences were exactly the kind of things that linked us together. I headed over to meet him at the library so that we could continue our own investigation. We had to figure out who the tele-porter person was in order to clear my name. Marlow had his laptop opened up and was typing away when I arrived.

"It's possible that our culprit is an undergrad or an extraordinary genius," Marlow said in a hushed voice, "but it's more likely that he is a senior or a grad student. I have all of the names of guys who are graduating or have recently graduated and have excelled in certain science fields." The list was large, understandably. Marlow's program ran through a bunch of faces and names.

"Do you recognize any of these?" I said quietly. Though the book shelves helped to buffer the sound, the high ceilings would echo if you talked too loudly.

"I only caught his profile for a split second."

"Could you tell if he was husky or skinny, short or tall?"

"Average height, average weight, average, average, average." Marlow blew a raspberry.

"Narrow the field to electronics and physics."

"I'll add juniors and sophomores."

"That's not narrowing the field. Wait stop." I pointed. "I know that guy. He hangs around Minji Park, Stella's gofer."

Marlow took a closer look. "That's Brandt Rheinhold. He's my biology lab partner and a part of the nerd squad. I can't imagine Brandt being our guy, but you just never know what kind of secrets people hold."

I checked the time on my phone. "I wish I could stay, Mars, but I have to get to the student building and lobby for my government seat."

His green-eyed gaze darted up at me. "You're still doing that?"

He knew my popularity had dropped like the New Years' ball in Time Square. I was sure that most of the students thought I should or would drop out, but I didn't like to quit something just because it was hard. "Yeah, I'm still doing it. Dakota is meeting me there so I gotta run."

Marlow's eyes widened at my announcement. Had Dakota not told him she was helping me?

Whatever. The dynamics of their relationship was none of my business.

I shifted my book bag strap over my shoulder, wrapped my scarf around my neck and quickly moved through the library.

Outside the wind was brisk and I pushed my scarf up over my mouth and nose. I welcomed the blast of warm air as I entered into the lobby of the student building. Stella was already there with Minji by her side, her table display ready with a new stack of promotional material. She spotted me and stared with narrow judgmental eyes. The room grew quiet as if she gave off a silent warning, like a dog whistle, signaling to everyone in the place that I had arrived. The frosty disapproval thickened as I continued toward the back of the room to claim my table. I sighed long and hard, highly tempted to turn around and run away.

As had become my norm, I kept my chin down, letting my hair fall, partially hiding my face. A classic ostrich move. If I couldn't see them, they couldn't see me.

It also made me peripherally blind, so I was completely unprepared when a set of hands pushed me from behind. I stumbled and crashed to the floor.

My face heated with humiliation and indignation as I stared up at my attacker. My ribs were still tender and I held in a moan.

Rudy Finch stood tall, legs spread, feet planted firmly and arms crossed. Deep lines etched a scowl on his face.

You could've heard a pin drop. Despite what people thought of me, there were a lot of shocked faces, but nobody stepped in to interfere.

"You killed Crystal Morrisette, bitch! You got no business running for student government."

"I'm not responsible for her death," I said as I pulled myself to my feet.

"It was your truck that hit her and you the one driving, so I'd say that makes you responsible."

I took a step back, my mind racing on how to diffuse this situation. "Let's let the courts decide."

Rudy made a move to shove me again, and next thing I knew, I'd taken hold of his arm and Rudy was lying flat on his back. An audible gasp filled the room.

He was up on his feet in an instant, spearing me with his glare. He took another step toward me and amazingly, an entire sequence of self-defense moves outlined themselves in my mind. I moved to a fighting position. I was ready.

Then suddenly a small body appeared between us and a dainty hand stretched out in protest.

"Stand down, Finch."

The appearance of Dakota and her authoritative stance shocked us all.

Rudy found it funny and laughed. "Okay, I'll stand down. No way your girl's going to win anyway."

He locked his dark-eyed gaze on me in a way that gave me chills. "See you later, killer."

Chapter Thirty

MARLOW

AFTER MY LAST class I headed to the dining hall, another brick building with long windows and high ceilings, my stomach urging me on. I scanned my student card at the door and the metal bar, which kept unregistered freeloaders out, opened to let me in. The place smelled *amazing*, and I hurried to get in line. Grilled pork chops with applesauce, buttered peas, and mashed potatoes and gravy. My stomach growled in anticipation.

I searched for an empty seat and spotted Zed waving his arm. He was with Brandt and Harland, and I joined them.

"Hey," I said, then dove straight into my meal.

Zed laughed, but I noticed that his and Brandt's plates were licked clean. Tall, skinny guys like us were always hungry. Harland moved slowly through the last of the peas rolling around on his plate. They were discussing the results of the Multi-Variable Calculus midterm, but I was too busy with my pork chops to pay attention.

After about ten minutes, though, my stomach signaled my brain that it would be okay to slow down.

"What do you guys know about teleportation?" I said. Something had been bothering me for a while, and now that Sage was safe and on the mend, my brain had room to pick at it.

Brandt leaned in. "You mean the *hypothetical possibility* of teleportation?"

"Yeah, yeah," I said, "the hypothetical possibility of teleportation."

"That would be an amazing science contest entry, huh?" Brandt said.

Harland coughed, his face turning a deep shade of red, and he beat at his chest. "Wrong w-way."

Zed commiserated. "Hate when that happens."

"Anyway," Brandt said, obviously a fan of the subject, "in theory, for teleportation to work, the object to be teleported would have to be completely disassembled, atom by atom, and then reassembled at alternate coordinates."

"Yeah, I know that," I said. "I guess what I'm wondering is, say for example, a man transports. Every atom in his body is disassembled and reassembled. In essence he dies and comes back to life, right?"

Brandt's thin lips slowly pulled up into a smile. "Yeah, that's what it would be like. Death and resurrection. Nothing short of playing God."

Harland started coughing again, and I pushed my glass of water his way. He took it without objection.

"Okay, Brandt, since you brought up God," my eyes darted to Zed then back to Brandt, "would that man's soul leave his body when he 'died', or would it go with him when he was 'resurrected'?"

Brandt leaned back and sniffed. "Oh man, heady stuff. Can't say I thought about that. I mean, I don't even believe in the concept of souls. We're just here until we're not."

"I'm sure the soul moves along with the body," Zed said. "If there is such a thing as a soul," he added with a glance at Brandt.

I stared back. "How can you be sure? You don't have any evidence to back it up."

Zed pointed his fork at me. "You don't have evidence to prove it doesn't."

"There has to be a way to find out."

"What does it matter? It's not like you believe in that anyway," Zed said. "Do you?"

Quite honestly, I wasn't sure. I hadn't been faced with the issue in such a personal way before. My mother came from a religious family. She was an intelligent person, yet I knew she believed.

Brandt interjected. "This is all theoretical, right?"

I'd forgotten momentarily that Zed and I weren't alone at the table. Getting carried away like that, revealing my hand to someone who could very well be on the suspect list was a dumb novice move.

"Yeah," I said. "Of course. Totally."

"Then theoretically," Brandt said, "I'd say if a man transports, and if he had a soul, the soul would ..."

Harland interjected, "Die."

"Hey, guys."

Our discussion was interrupted by the arrival of Dakota. She pulled out the chair beside me, and leaned in for a kiss.

"What are you guys talking about so intensely?"

"It's nothing," I said quickly. "Just a hypothetical science thing."

"My favorite kind," she said, smiling. "What's the hypothesis?"

Brandt answered, "Marlow asked if a man were to teleport from one place to another, would he lose his soul, if he had a soul, in the process?"

"Wow," Dakota said. "You guys are the kings of small talk." She cut a piece off her pork chop and took a bite. "So what's the conclusion?"

"No conclusion since it's just hypoth..."

Brandt cut me off. "Zed thinks the soul would go with the man and I think he'd lose it, if in fact a religious 'soul' even exists." He pushed back from the table. "Anyway, dudes and dudette, I'm flying."

Harland took opportunity to leave at the same time, but said nothing. Not one for social graces, that guy.

"What brought up this topic?" Dakota asked. I knew she was just trying to make conversation, but since I *had* actually teleported, I was kind of worried about the state of my soul. I couldn't talk to her about that, though. She'd think me certifiably crazy.

I shrugged lazily. "Ah, just nerds being nerds."

"That's us," Zed said. "Just nerds being nerds."

"You don't have to repeat what I said."

"I was just trying to support you, dude."

"Hey!" Dakota said. "I don't know what's going on here, but can you cool your jets for just a moment? I have something to tell you."

"Both of us?" I asked.

"Well, it involves Sage, and since you're both friends of hers."

My head snapped up. "What happened?" I said sharply. "Is she okay?"

Dakota blinked at my reaction. "Rudy Finch pushed her down in the student building and accused her of killing that media girl."

"Garvin's TA *pushed* her down?" I could feel the veins in my neck throbbing.

"Yeah, I saw everything. He came up from behind her and gave her a two-handed shove. When she stood up, he tried to shove her again, but the weirdest thing. She twisted his arm backward and he was on the floor."

"Then what happened?" Zed said.

"He jumped to his feet and started toward her again. Then..."

"Then what?" My knees were jumping under the table. "Is she okay?"

"I stepped in between them and put a stop to it."

That was the absolute last thing I could've guessed she would say. "Seriously? Just like that?"

"I think it was the shock factor," Dakota said. "He didn't expect someone like me to step up."

Zed laughed. "Whoa, our girl's a badass!"

Dakota smiled at Zed and blushed at his compliment.

"I think they both just needed a way to stop things and neither was going to take the first step," she said. "Rudy started laughing and then left. I helped Sage set up and we handed out flyers."

"And Sage's okay?"

"Yes. She's okay. I'm not sure if her performance won the crowd's respect or made them fear her, but she gave away a lot of flyers."

I was a bull, snorting short heavy breaths through my nose, head down and horns ready to spear the hot-headed TA. I jumped up from the table. "I'm going to kill him."

Zed scampered to my side. "Steady dude. Guys like us use our wits not our brawn. Guys like us don't do well in prisons."

Dakota tugged on my arm and gave me a stern look. "I told you she's okay, Marlow." She was frowning at me again. Somehow I always managed to ruin the mood when I was with her.

Chapter Thirty-One

THE PAWN SHOP was locked up tight. Metal screens like prison issued grates covered the exterior side of the windows that flashed big neon signs: "We Buy Gold and Silver" and "Instant Cash".

He didn't have to worry about locks. Once he'd established the co-ordinates of the interior, he mapped out the entrance so he wouldn't accidentally land on deer horns or a glass table, and simply teleported inside.

He wore an oversized hoodie with the hood pulled over his head, and made sure not to look up at the security cameras. He'd made note of them previously when he came to sign his lease.

A nervous giggle escaped his lips as he took in all the pawned treasures, and it occurred to him he'd never have to buy a single thing again. The best cat burglar in history—he'd be unstoppable!

He ran a gloved finger along the top of the jewelry cabinet filled with every kind of gold and silver trinket. It was locked, but he was certain he could find the key. Lambert wasn't that creative.

A gun cabinet hung behind the cash counter. This was why he'd come. He wanted a gun. Again, he just had to find the key to the cabinet, which was likely stored in Lambert's office at the back. Best to get to it.

His path took him past the sports section and he stopped when he spotted the hockey equipment. There were sticks and masks and jerseys. He'd grown up watching the game on TV and dreamed of making the NHL, but his mom said hockey was a sport for rich kids and put him in soccer instead.

Turned out he wasn't that athletic, but it burned in his gut like fire to let the dream die.

He picked up a stick and tested it out with an imaginary puck. *He shoots, he scores!* There were a number of hockey masks hanging from hooks on the wall, and an old-style one with an image of a skull painted on it in black caught his eye. He snatched it and put it on.

He felt powerful and invincible. He faced one of the security cameras and pounded his chest like an ape.

With mask on and hockey stick in hand, he entered the office. He dug through the desk and found nothing.

The file cabinets were equally uncooperative. With growing agitation he ransacked the room, clearing everything on Lambert's desk onto the floor. He let out a growl of frustration.

He must've thrown a security switch, because standing in the doorway was Lambert himself. "Hey!"

Swinging the hockey stick like a sword, he clipped the old man in the head. Lambert tripped over the trash can and landed hard on his back. Blood flowed from the cut on his cheek.

"The key to the gun case?"

The old man trembled but said nothing.

He placed the blade of the stick along the man's throat and pressed.

"Under the carpet in the corner under the window, there's a safe."

"Combination?"

Lambert croaked out the numbers. He struck the man again, and his head bobbed to the side.

He found the key and claimed a gun, disappearing just as the cops arrived.

Chapter Thirty-Two

MARLOW

AFTER EVERYTHING I'd been through in my freshman year, I'd developed an interest in criminology, so I decided to take CRIM 101 as one of my electives. It wasn't unexpected to see Sage had come to the same conclusion, but I was surprised that, after mentioning my course selection to Zed and Dakota, they had both decided to take it too.

"Thanks to you," Zed had said, "I've come in contact with the criminal mind. I think it would do me well to understand it better." He added morbidly, "Just in case."

"My dad's a forensic pathologist," Dakota said. "Who knows, maybe I'll decide to follow in his footsteps." It was hard to imagine my pint-size, pink-haired girlfriend cutting up cadavers.

The four of us taking the same class caused me to experience an irrational amount of anxiety. The other three didn't seem to be affected in the same way. Zed and Sage had forged a friendship over the summer, so seeing them together was only sort of weird for me. It was the close proximity of Dakota and Sage— to each other and to me—that made me break out in a cold sweat.

Criminology was taught in a building across campus so I only had a short window to get there after my chemistry lab. I had to catch a university bus heading toward the park, then hoof it two blocks to the sociology building. I slowed down the block before it to catch my breath—hello, I was going to sit close to two beautiful girls, both of whom I was attracted to, and I didn't want to arrive out of breath looking like I was about to puke.

Sage got there when I did.

"Hey," she said without smiling.

"Hey," I said back. "Dakota told me what happened yesterday. Are you okay?"

Her mouth twitched. "Do I look okay?"

"Well, yeah, you look great, actually."

She looked at me and said stiffly, "Thanks."

"Dakota said you had that idiot on the ground. Way to go."

"That part was a little surprising."

Nudging her elbow playfully I said, "Have you been watching Bruce Lee on the sly?"

She didn't smile back, just walked on ahead. I got the sense that she was put out with me. I probably should've called her or texted her as soon as I heard about the incident, but Dakota had been with me until late last night and I knew how sensitive she was about me interacting too much with Sage. By the time Dakota left, it felt weird to start calling because I had left it so long.

With Dakota and Sage I felt like I was in a perpetual lose/lose situation.

The class was held in a small lecture theater. Zed, being a creature of habit, always sat in the same seat, right hand side, three rows from the front, second chair from the aisle. Sage usually took the empty seat beside him, while Dakota and I chose anything free in the rows behind them. I was strategic about this because I couldn't stand having Sage watching me and Dakota from behind. I'd much rather have the opportunity to observe her.

Zed always arrived early, since he had a math class prior, which was closer than my chemistry class. Today Dakota had made it earlier too. She was sitting in Sage's chair, giving Zed rapt attention.

"How many theoretical physicists does it take to change a light bulb?" he said.

Dakota's eyes twinkled with amusement. "How many?"

"Two. One to hold the bulb and one to rotate the universe."

Dakota giggled and I rolled my eyes at Sage. We took a step closer.

"Photon checks into a hotel," Dakota said to Zed. "The bellhop asks, 'Can I help you with your luggage?' It replies, 'I don't have any. I'm traveling light.'"

Zed chortled.

I paused mid-step. I'd heard Zed's joke a hundred times, but Dakota had never told a joke in my presence. Never to me.

"Is something wrong?" Sage said.

I forced a smile. "No."

Sage accepted my short answer and continued ahead of me. "Hey, guys," she announced. Dakota looked up at her in surprise, then scampered out of the chair beside Zed. She smiled at him before joining me.

"Where do you want to sit?" she asked, like nothing monumental had happened at all.

Chapter Thirty-Three

SAGE

THERE WAS no doubt in my mind that Dakota would've told Marlow about my encounter with Rudy Finch yesterday. Did I mean so little to Marlow that he couldn't spare a minute to ask me about it? Especially since we're in the middle of an investigation?

My feelings were hurt and that made me feel stupid and vulnerable. And mad. Hot emotions and energy that I funneled into my search for info on Rudy Finch.

What an asshole! Professor Garvin had to be blind to hire him as his assistant. I had a good mind to file a report. I should anyway. The police would charge him with assault, fingerprint him and put him behind bars.

See? If Marlow had called me, we would've

worked out our next move together. Instead I was breaking into Rudy's dorm room by myself.

Somehow I knew how to pick a lock. I wondered where all these latent skills were coming from. Possibly I actually learned something from all those crime novels I read when I wasn't actually trying to solve a crime.

As my fingers worked with the bobby pin I'd pulled out of my hair, my mind reviewed what I had learned from my online search.

Rudy was a rich kid whose family owned one of the mansions along Detroit River, which would explain why he didn't have to share a dorm room like most everyone else. He was known for his short temper if you could go by the comments on his Facebook page. He was at DU working on his masters degree in physics and managed to snag the TA gig.

The lock system clicked and I was surprised my efforts had actually worked. Checking to make sure the coast was still clear, I pushed Rudy's door open, slipped inside and almost had a heart attack.

The room was a shrine to Crystal Morrisette. Posters of the well-endowed woman papered the wall. One of the larger ones was even signed. Crystal figurines peppered the desk and shelf space. There was a stack of small cardboard shipping boxes and paper packing material. Had Rudy been sending Crystal gifts?

The guy was clearly obsessed. No wonder he was so upset by her death.

Or was he was so upset because he'd inadvertently killed her and needed someone to blame?

Was Rudy Finch our guy?

Or, maybe that scene in the student building was just a show to deflect his guilt onto me. He was working on his master's degree in physics so obviously he had an above average IQ. Had he been monitoring traffic on the forest road somehow? Did he know when he teleported Crystal Morrisette that she would be hit by a vehicle? Maybe he had already killed her before-hand, and needed to cover it up?

There were stacks of textbooks on Rudy's desk, as well as an open notebook. I flipped through the pages, but it appeared to be nothing more than a class assign-ment. Rudy wasn't exactly a clean freak. It appeared he just dropped his clothes as he removed them, like a male version of Nora.

Even though he didn't have to share, the second bed remained, though you'd hardly know it for all the stuff stacked on it. I wasn't sure what I hoped to find. Something incriminating, but what?

I stiffened at the sound of a key in the lock. The

door opened a crack and Rudy's conversation with another guy filtered in.

"My p-paper doesn't deserve this m-mark."

"You're right," Rudy said. "I was being generous. It deserved lower."

I scoured the room searching desperately for a place to hide. Rudy's room was on the third floor, so jumping out the window wasn't an option. But, he was such a slob that I should be able to work it to my advantage.

The angry student shouted, "I'm takin' this up w- with G-Garvin!"

"I know what the man expects from his students and what you produced wasn't it."

"You'll b-be s-sorry!"

Rudy gave a mocking laugh. "Yeah. I'll b-be s-sorry."

I collapsed to the floor and rolled under the unused bed just as Rudy slammed the door. My heart beat hard and fast against my ribs. I was trapped like a rabbit. Plus it stank. Rudy stored his shoes here and the foot odor was sharp enough to kill a cat. I carefully moved my hand up to my face to cover my mouth and nose.

From here I could see the casters of the desk chair roll back and Rudy sinking into it. I heard the zipper of his backpack followed by the rapid clicking of keys on his laptop. Oh God. I hoped he wasn't delving into a long assignment. My legs were already starting to cramp.

Rudy farted and belched and I could picture him scratching his armpits like an ape.

Please leave, please leave, please leave.

My nose itched from the dust bunnies and my mouth was dry as cotton. A tickle started at the back of my throat and I fought the urge to cough. It was tortuous.

Finally, Rudy got up from his chair. A minute later I heard him peeing in the bathroom. Could I escape while he was in there? No, I hadn't heard him shut the door.

When he came back into the room he sat on the empty bed—was there a spot not covered with his crap? —and the mattress sank low enough to touch my back. I was cramped, dry mouthed, and now suffering a bout of claustrophobia.

Then his fingers fumbled under the bed. I pushed the nearest shoe until his fingers touched, held my breath, hoping it was the one he was looking for.

He put it on and I quickly found the matching shoe, placing it in the path of his searching fingers.

I couldn't imagine what Rudy would do if he

discovered me. Likely my body would show up in the canal sometime tomorrow. I forced myself to stay still, holding my breath and covering my mouth. The door slammed shut and I counted to ten just to make sure he didn't swing back inside for something he forgot.

Then I got the hell out of there.

Chapter Thirty-Four

MARLOW

I STARED AT HER TEXT.

Sage: Mars! Meet me in the courtyard. It's urgent.

"Is everything okay?" Dakota whispered, eyeing my warily. We were working on class assignments in the library with Zed, who stopped typing at the sound of Dakota's voice.

"Uh, yeah, fine. But, I have to take this."

I felt the lazer stare of disapproval from both Dakota and Zed as I left. Within minutes I was at the courtyard. Sage approached from the opposite side. From a distance it would have probably looked like the two of us jogging to meet each other were lovers who hadn't seen each other in ages. Minus a lip lock, which, unfortunately, our greeting didn't end in.

"What is it?" I struggled to manage my breathing. "What's wrong?"

Her face was pink with excitement. "I think I know who the killer is."

"Really? Who?"

"Rudy Finch."

"Garvin's TA? What makes you think that?"

"His room is a shrine to Crystal Morrisette. There are pictures of her all over his wall and he's been sending her crystal figurines."

I ducked lower to catch her eyes. "Wait. How do you know this?"

Her gaze flittered to the ground before she found my eyes again. "I kind of broke in. I picked the lock."

Sage was full of surprises, and I wasn't exactly happy about this one. "You picked the lock?"

"Yeah."

"How did you know how to do that?"

"I'm not sure. I think I just got lucky."

"Did anyone see you? This could be really dangerous."

"No." She hesitated like there was more, then added, "He showed up when I was there, but I hid under the bed until he left."

I flailed my arms in disbelief. I wanted to shake her. "Sage! Do you know what could've happened to you if he'd found you there?"

"He didn't find me, okay? The point is he bullied me yesterday because of Crystal Morrisette and today I discovered his obsession with her. I think he could be our guy. We need to call Jack."

I pulled out my phone, dismayed by how my hand shook. I clenched my jaw tight to keep the anger I felt at Sage for needlessly putting herself in danger like that from lashing out at her.

Jack answered on the second ring. "Hey, Marlow. What's up?"

"We have a lead on a possible suspect."

"Okay, let's not do this over the phone. I'll be there in thirty minutes."

That gave Sage and me time to grab a couple of coffees on our way, and time for me to cool down. I didn't think I could say anything to her without it sounding like a scolding.

It was a quiet walk to the main parking lot and the tension in my chest eased somewhat by the time we got there. Jack was already there and I hopped in the passenger seat of his gray sedan while Sage slid in the back.

Jack gave us both a look. "Okay, let me have it."

I updated him on Sage's suspicions and the condition of Rudy Finch's dorm room. Jack cast a backwards glance at Sage and arched a brow at her brazen B&E,

but said nothing about it. He started the car and pulled into the flow of traffic.

"Where are we going?" I asked.

"You still want to know where I work?"

Really? He was going to tell us about his secret job? "Sure."

"Before I can take you there, you'll have to be willing to sign a strict confidentiality agreement."

Made sense to me. "Of course."

"When I say strict, I mean more than you probably think."

"Like what?" I said.

He glanced at me briefly. "You must agree to having your memories of the organization and everything unusual to do with this case erased, once we get the guy."

Sage leaned forward, poking her dark head between us. "Seriously?"

"Seriously."

"Why would we agree to that?" I asked. "It's absurd."

"It is. But unless you agree, there is nothing more I can tell you. I'll just turn around and take you back."

"How do you isolate memories to erase?" Sage said. "I didn't know something like that could be done."

"I can't even tell you that until you agree."

I twisted to look at Sage and assessed her body

language. I was hoping she'd be sitting back, arms crossed, gazing blankly out the window, but her expression was eager and she bounced with excitement, arms resting on the back of Jack's seat. "I agree," she said.

I couldn't very well let her go ahead without me, so I added reluctantly, "Me too."

"Okay, are you going to tell us about the secret organization now?" Sage asked.

Jack muttered, "Yup," then stayed silent for the next two minutes. Waiting for him to explain what had been such a big mystery between us tested my patience.

"Can you tell us anything now?"

"Okay, okay," he let out a low chuckle like he got a kick out of pulling my chain. "I work for a sub-government agency called CISUE."

"See sue?" I asked

"Spelt C.I.S.U.E., Central intelligence for Special or Unusual Events. Our department investigates the extraordinary and unexplainable phenomenon."

"Like the TV show *Fringe*?" Sage asked.

"Yeah, kind of like that," Jack said. "Except without the crazy scientist."

"Cool," I said, legitimately impressed.

Jack smirked. "You guys know a little about extraordinary and unusual events."

We were almost out of city limits when Jack pulled

into an underground parking garage. The building overhead was nondescript and a bit run down; it could've been any old warehouse. A good façade for a secret agency.

The hallway inside had plain white walls and worn gray carpet. There was one elevator, which we got into, and Jack pushed the number five. The scene on the fifth floor looked like it could've been the office area of any random business, with people sitting at computer terminals and talking on phones. Our presence earned a few seconds of note and a couple people even waved at us.

Jack took us through to another elevator. He placed a thumb on a security pad, and then the elevator door opened. "The sixth floor isn't accessible to everyone," he explained. I understood why when the doors opened to let us out again. Before us was a special ops station—NCIS type. Big screens, 3D animation, personnel with headphones and computer keyboards, and a wall of monitors flashing satellite images from all corners of the world. Sage and I both gaped at it all.

Jack dropped us off in what appeared to be an ordinary office conference room with windows that looked out to the control area where all the activity was being monitored. My leg bounced with nerves as if it had a mind of its own. Sage laid a hand on my knee to still it and my heart almost stopped. I glanced down at her fingers and then up at her face. She quickly moved her hand away.

Jack returned and four people entered behind him.

"These are agents Seaway, Black and Kato," Jack said. Agent Seaway was in her mid forties, with dull brown hair cut short; Agent Black was a bit younger with a Mad Men look; and Agent Kato was Asian, not much older than Sage and me, and shared Sage's preference for fashion eyewear. She adjusted silver frames and smiled at us.

Jack added, "Black and Seaway are field agents, and Kato is tech."

Behind them was an older African American man with short-cut gray hair. Jack introduced him as Dr. Abe Turner, Chief of CISUE. Unlike the agents who immediately settled into the boardroom chairs, Dr. Turner circled around the table to where Sage and I were seated. He shook our hands in succession, his gaze lingering on Sage.

"Welcome," he said. "So good to see you."

Then he sat across from Sage, his deep-brown eyes smiling at her with affection. It made me wonder if there was a connection there. He tented his hands and addressed us, "When Jack suggested we bring you two in on this investigation, I was resistant. The people and situations we deal with at CISUE are often volatile and dangerous. I certainly don't want to purposely put young people in harm's way. However, as Jack pointed out, this case seems to have drawn the two of you in, despite my objections. We can better protect you if we have you working with us."

"Let us know how we can help," Sage said. I was unhappy with how eager she was to dive into something Dr. Turner had just described as "volatile and dangerous."

"Of course," Dr. Turner said. "How about we review the case first. Marlow, why don't you tell us how things started?"

I brought everyone up to date on Sage's accident, the death of Crystal Morrisette and my teleportation experience.

"Each time he teleports an energy signal is given off," Agent Kato said. "The code is unlike anything we've ever monitored before, so it immediately caught our attention. We picked up the unusual activity on the night of the accident. There were ten other occasions previously, two per day on five different occasions. Each set of two were only minutes apart, between one and five.

"What was unusual about that night was the odd number. A set of two, then a single transmission, then another set of two."

"I'm guessing Crystal Morrisette was teleported out and back," Sage said, "and when the perpetrator saw that Crystal was dead, he panicked and teleported her back."

I agreed. "That would explain why we didn't see Crystal's body right away. I thought I missed it because I was distracted by the accident and worried about Sage, but the body wasn't there at that moment to see."

"If you're picking up the signals," Sage said, "why can't you get a lock on him?"

Agent Black spoke up. "When the suspect teleports, the sign patch is only a split second, not long enough for us to get a precise location, only the general vicinity. It makes it hard for us to nab the guy."

Jack leaned back in his chair and threaded his fingers. His lips worked as his eyes narrowed, a tell I recognized from before. He was about to say something he didn't want to.

"This is where you two come in. The suspect is either a student or faculty member or maybe even someone who works at the University. Someone with a high IQ, but who feels ostracized, marginalized, and has some kind of ax to grind. We need you to keep your eyes and ears open on campus and report back on anything unusual or suspicious."

"Can you think of anything?" Seaway said. She

stared at us with steely-gray eyes, and I didn't doubt she was serious about her job.

"Rudy Finch has a way of ostracizing himself," Sage said. "He has a temper. He doesn't share his dorm room with anyone. He lords his authority as a teachers assistant over the other students. You should've heard how he spoke to one of them." Sage recited the conversation Rudy had with the person in the hall outside his dorm. "Plus, he was obsessed with Crystal Morrisette."

"Rudy Finch makes a good suspect," Jack said. "We need more Intel on him. We want you to watch him carefully, do some digging, maybe question other students about him. Something that could point to where he's moved his operations."

I shared a look with Sage and we both nodded. "Okay."

"But please," Dr. Turner interjected, "be careful. Don't take any unnecessary risks."

"We'll be careful," Sage said.

The agents left and Dr. Turner said good-bye. Again he cupped Sage's hands, holding on for a second longer than required.

"What else goes on here?" Sage said when we were alone with Jack. "In a weird way I feel like I've been here before.""

Jack's chin snapped up in surprise. "Really?"

"Probably just reminds you of something you've seen on TV," I said.

"Actually, Marlow," Jack said as he leaned forward, resting his elbows on the table, "her instincts are right. You've both been here before. In fact you've both been here more than once."

That would explain Dr. Turner's familiar behavior. Something had happened that made him feel close to us, especially Sage.

"And you've wiped our memories," I said. It bothered me, though I knew we must've had agreed to it, like we did this time."

"Yes, for your own protection," Jack said. "There's a lot of sensitive information here, and if it and you ended up in the wrong hands... So it's best if you don't know. And we don't want to sway the direction of your life prematurely. Once you've graduated from University and you know this is the kind of life you want to lead, then we can talk about recruitment. That's our policy."

"Hey, is this why I knew how to pick that lock, or how to flip Rudy onto his back?" Sage said.

Jack nodded. "In the other times you've been here you've had opportunity to train with our self-defense team and spy technician."

I was stunned by this revelation, and I had to admit

it was kind of cool. We were spies and secret agents, so secret *we* didn't even know it.

Thinking back it made sense now how someone like me, a skinny non-active dude, could do some of the things I'd done.

"In fact," Jack said, "I'd like you to take a couple hours this afternoon to refresh your skills. They might come in handy."

Chapter Thirty-Five

SAGE

IVAN WAS OUR SELF-DEFENSE INSTRUCTOR. He had short dark hair, a closely trimmed beard on a nice-looking face, and was toned and limber, bouncing on the balls of his feet like he was walking on air.

He saw us and smiled. "Hey guys, nice to see you again."

I glanced at Marlow and we shared an understanding. We didn't know who this guy was.

"Right, you guys don't remember me. Hello. I'm Ivan, and I'll be your self-defence instructor today." He addressed us formally like we were first-timers in a private class, then snickered at his own joke.

"Okay, let's begin with warming up. We don't want to blow out your muscles on the first day." He led us through a series of body stretches, lunges, and toe touching. I winced a little when the muscles around my ribs protested, but at least the stitches from my forehead and wrist were gone. I had two pink scars to forever remind me to appreciate my life.

I had to smile at how Marlow pinched his face. He wasn't naturally athletic; his long limbs and pointy joints reminded me of a grasshopper.

Ivan clapped his hands. "Alright, let's see how your muscle memory does." He pointed to a kick bag. "Take it away, Sage."

I approached the bag nervously, unsure what to do. Ivan encouraged me by punching the air. Feeling bashfully self-conscious in front of Marlow, I hit the bag with a tentative right-hand punch. Then a left, another right, another left. Harder and harder, with growing energy. My body just moved without me telling it, switching to elbow strikes. Right elbow to the stomach, backward hammer strike to the kidneys. I repeated it on the other side of the bag. From there I stepped into round-housed kicks with my right leg—yes, that was what it was called, a round house kick—and followed it with a sequence of other kicks, front and back and ending with a final roundhouse kick.

I stepped back, wiping sweat off my forehead. Ivan applauded. Marlow stared, mouth open, like he couldn't believe what he'd just witnessed. I was shocked myself at what I had done, somehow knowing exactly what to do without having learned technique.

"You're up, Marlow," Ivan said. Marlow approached the bag looking as worried as I had felt at first. "You can do this, Mars," I encouraged.

He poked his forehead like he often did when he forgot he wasn't wearing lenses, and I held in a smile.

"You're a tough act to follow," he said.

Ivan jabbed the air the same way he had done with me, encouraging Marlow to step up. And then Marlow started punching.

Once he let himself go, he actually beat the crap out of the bag—hard fist strikes and strong repetitive kicks. It was mesmerizing. Marlow looked really hot in action. No longer an awkward grasshopper, but a lithe ninja. I felt my face flush and I had to turn away.

"Good job, both of you," Ivan said. "Are you feeling warmed up now?"

We both nodded, but I couldn't look Marlow in the eye.

Ivan was oblivious to my discomfort. He instructed us to stand about six feet apart, facing each other. "Marlow, you are approaching Sage in an aggressive manner. You reach for her shoulders."

The warmth of Marlow's hands and our close approximation caused my heart to pitter-patter. I automatically stepped in with my right foot, grabbed the cuff of his T-shirt with my left hand, and the area near his collar with my right. I pulled him to me, my left elbow up, twisting my arm as if I needed to look at my watch, and knocking Marlow slightly off balance. I released the collar of his shirt and brought my arm up under his armpit. I stepped back with my left foot, twisting my hips and bent over, pulling Marlow over my shoulder and onto his back. It took less than three seconds.

"That's what I did to Rudy Finch the other day."

Marlow stood and stared at me with his mouth hanging open.

"Okay, Marlow," Ivan said. "You're walking down the street, minding your own business, and someone comes up from behind and puts you in a chokehold. What do you do?" Ivan looked at me and chin-nodded toward Marlow. I was shorter than Marlow, but I could still reach up if I went on my tiptoes and grab him around the neck. Marlow immediately ducked his chin before I could get a good grip. He reached over with his left hand to pull on my elbow, stepped behind me with his left leg, and twisted out. Since he still had a grip on my elbow, he wrenched it behind my back and dropped his weight on the back of my knees.

"Ow!"

Marlow broke his hold and helped me up, worry in his eyes. "Did I hurt you?"

"I'm okay," I said rubbing my arm. "No worries."

"You got to expect to end up with a few bruises in this class," Ivan said. "It's the only way to learn."

He pivoted toward me. "Sage, you're wearing your hair in a ponytail. What do you do if some guy grabs your ponytail and pulls?"

I walked across the room like I was minding my own business passing Marlow who was pretending to be hiding in the shadows. He reached for my ponytail and pulled. My left hand flew like a windmill behind me hitting Marlow's wrist like a board. He lost his grip on my ponytail, but I stepped in continuing to block his arm and thrust a flattened fist with my knuckles jabbing his throat. Marlow dropped to his knees on the ground gasping, and I was horrified.

"Marlow?" I glared daggers at Ivan. "We can't keep hurting each other like this."

I helped Marlow up as he got his breath back. He rubbed his neck and looked at me like I scared him.

"I'm sorry, Marlow."

"It's okay," he said, his voice raspy. After a few seconds he added, "I'm actually really glad to see how capable you are at taking a creep down."

"Alright, let's do one more," Ivan said, "and I'll let you get back to your day. Sage, you've stumbled to the ground and your attacker is on top of you. This is a classic rape scenario. What do you do?"

Marlow and I exchanged a round of rapid blinking as understanding dawned on us. Ivan wanted me to lie down and Marlow was supposed to hover over me, his knees between mine. Neither of us made a move.

"Come on, guys." Ivan clapped his hands to spook us into motion. "This is a real situation that happens to women every day."

Slowly I reached for the ground and lowered myself to my back. I could tell Marlow was nervous by how his eyes darted around at everything but my face and how his fingers tapped against his thighs. He glanced at Ivan one more time and Ivan nodded him on. Marlow fell to his knees and shifted in between my legs. His Adam's apple bobbed, and I dry swallowed along with him. Awkward didn't even begin to describe how uncomfortable this was.

"Okay, Marlow. You need to pin her arms down."

I lifted my arms up beside my head and waited for Marlow to grab them. I could feel the weight of his body on me, his hands on my arms, his face six inches from mine. If this were a romantic movie, this would be the scene where the lovers finally kiss with passionate abandonment. This wasn't a movie and we had an impatient instructor to pull me out of any romantic fantasy.

"Sage, what would you do?" Ivan barked.

I thrust my hips up, lifting my right leg and

dropped it in front of his chest over both his arms, jerking him off balance, and forcing him to release his hold on me. I twisted sideways and rolled. Up on my feet. Stomp on his ankle. Run away.

I didn't want to actually hurt him and I held back some of my weight. Apparently not enough.

Marlow groaned. "I'm tired of being beat up by a girl."

Chapter Thirty-Six

MARLOW

WHILE JACK WAS DRIVING us back to campus Sage got a call from her mechanic that her truck was ready.

"Jack, would you mind dropping me off at Rod's Auto Mechanics?" she asked.

"I can drop off both of you there," Jack said. "I'm not comfortable dropping you off on your own. Not with a lunatic on the loose."

"I agree," I said, crossing my arms in an attempt to make me look like a wall she couldn't budge. "If you want to pick up your truck, I'm going to tag along."

Sage eyed my posture with amusement and said airily, "You can come." Jack twisted his body to look at Sage after we pulled into the shop. "CISUE has taken care of your bill."

Sage sat up straight in surprise. "Really? Are you sure?"

"Yeah. You wouldn't have gotten into that accident if it weren't for an unexplained or unusual circumstance, and that's what we are all about."

Sage broke into a smile that made her eyes sparkle. "Thank the agency for me."

She burst into a child-like squeal when she saw her truck parked in front of the garage. We walked to it and she stroked the hood. "Hey, Boy Toy. I've missed you."

I stared at her incredulously. "You named your truck Boy Toy?"

"Yup. I'm off flesh and blood men."

I scoffed. "I don't believe you."

"It's true. And I couldn't be happier."

She did look pretty happy, but still, her announcement bugged me.

The mechanic smirked at her childlike joy as he gave her the keys. "She's got a new bumper, new airbags and a new driver's seat," he said proudly. "We gave her a tune-up, cleaned her up nice."

"It looks great!" Sage said. "Thank-you!"

We hopped in and headed back to DU.

"This is a nice ride, Sage," I said.

"Thanks. I think so." She stroked the steering wheel with exaggeration.

"But there's no way I'm going to refer to it as—"

"BOY TOY!" Sage laughed and I laughed with her. I missed seeing this happy side of her.

Her smile fell into something more solemn. "Mars, I feel like I want to go back to the scene of the accident."

"No need. Jack and I have already done it."

She shot me a quick look. "You have?"

"I should've told you. You were still in the hospital. Nothing to report though, we didn't find any evidence."

"I'd still like to go back. If not for the case, just for my own sake. I don't know if that makes sense."

"It makes perfect sense. Do you want to go now?"

"You don't have to come."

"Jack would kill me if I let you go alone."

"Yeah, you're right." She made a U-turn and headed north toward the forest and the bush party.

I couldn't let Sage go back to the scene of the accident alone, but I also couldn't keep leaving Dakota hanging. I sent her a quick text telling her my dad arrived unannounced and we were having a late lunch. A half-truth. It made the juices in my gut swirl. I hated how I kept lying to her.

Sage watched me as I tucked my phone back in my pocket. Her mouth moved and I thought she was going to ask me about Dakota, but instead she asked, "What does it feel like to teleport?"

I tapped my fingers on the door rest. "Well, at first I was just freaked out. I didn't understand what was happening. One moment I was outside in the forest and the next I was inside a small, dark space that smelled funky. The next thing I knew, I was back on the forest road. I thought I'd been drugged or something, or that I'd had some kind of hallucination. I really didn't understand what was going on until later."

"What did it feel like physically?"

"It felt like an electric shock. Uncomfortable, but not that painful."

Sage was focusing more on the ditch than the road, searching for the tree she hit. I noticed something lying on the middle of the road before she did.

"Sage, slow down." I pointed. "What's that?"

She hit the brakes. "I don't know. Is it a deer? Or a dog?"

As we got closer though, I knew it was worse than that.

"It looks like a body."

Sage paled and her hands trembled on the steering wheel. "Oh no."

She parked the truck on the edge of the road, and we jumped out. It was definitely a body, a man lying flat on his back with his hands resting on his belly like he was simply sleeping.

"You've got to be kidding," Sage said.

I couldn't believe my eyes either. The dead man was Rudy Finch.

"I guess this eliminates him from our suspect list," I said.

"I know, damn."

I called Jack to report it and he said to stay with the body until his team got there.

"It's kind of creepy," Sage said, her voice catching. "Out in the middle of nowhere with him... dead."

I had to agree, but also somehow I was not surprised.

We stared at the dead man on the road.

Sage squatted for a closer look. "He was stabbed."

I was on high alert. Our guy could be lurking in the forest somewhere watching.

I recalled the footage of the pawnshop break in Jack had shown us. The guy didn't face the camera until he'd put on the skull-painted hockey mask, and wielded the hockey stick like a sword on the unconscious Mr. Lambert. At least Lambert had survived.

"First an accidental death, then a physical beating with a hockey stick, and now a stabbing death. The guy's rage is accelerating."

"That's assuming that our teleporter is responsible for this," Sage said.

"Yes. True, but only our teleporter would know about these exact coordinates."

Sage stood, frowning. "Yeah you're right."

"Teleportation must affect him psychologically," I said. "I mean, every time he teleports his cells are disassembled and then reassembled. You know how complicated the brain is. Even the most minute change could alter his personality."

"You seem okay."

"I only teleported once."

"Twice, actually. There and back."

I felt sick to my stomach. Soulless? "Yeah, well, I'm probably an even bigger geek as a result."

"It's likely altering him physically as well," Sage said. "Let's take a look around to see if we can find any new evidence."

I didn't like the idea of leaving her side, but rationally, the more she moved about, the less likely it was that the guy could grab her co-ordinates—if that was how it worked—and assuming he was monitoring this area. Probably a good thing for me to shuffle around too.

"Are these his footprints?" Sage pointed to heel imprints in the gravel. "A sign of a scuffle?"

"More like drag marks. I bet Rudy was already dead before he was brought here. I wonder why our guy killed him? What was his motive?"

Sage continued to scope the ground. "Jealousy? Maybe he's been to Rudy's dorm room."

"I wonder if he really meant to kill Crystal. I think he's angry that she's dead and that's what started this."

"What makes you say that?" Sage asked, eyeing me.

"I know they were acquainted. He worked across the alley from where she lived, and he was in possession of one of her crystal figurines. She was a beautiful woman, so no doubt he was attracted to her. She must've done something to aggravate him or to hurt him or to make him mad, and he lashed out."

"It's a good hypothesis, Mars."

"It's not a stretch to assume he was already on the edge emotionally and that something pushed him over.

Sage crouched down and picked at something in the dirt. Whatever she found was small enough to fit on the tip of her finger.

"What is it?" I asked

"Maybe nothing, but it looks like a paint chip."

I leaned in for a closer look. "Give it to Jack when he gets here."

We turned to the sound of an approaching vehicle. Jack's car rolled up, and he along with Agents Black and Seaway got out and strolled toward Rudy Finch's body. Black examined the body while Seaway searched the area.

Jack shook his head. "I hate it when they're so young."

Sage offered up the evidence on her fingertip. "I found this on the road. I don't know if it's anything but it might have come from our suspect."

Seaway, overhearing, pulled out a small evidence bag from her pocket, opened it, and Sage dropped the paint chip in.

"Good eye, kiddo," Jack said. "We'll get it analyzed and let you know."

Chapter Thirty-Seven

SAGE

THERE WASN'T MUCH that Marlow and I could do once the CISUE team got there, so we said goodbye to Jack and headed back to the university.

I didn't think I could concentrate on calculus. I wanted to talk this out, debrief. "I don't know about you, but I'm not ready to go back to class."

Marlow's fingers drummed on the top of his thighs. "Me neither."

"Harvey's?" I suggested? "I really could use a steak sandwich about now."

"Sounds good."

Harvey's Pub, located just outside the boundaries of the university, was a popular hangout for DU students. It had a dark, dusky ambience, with dim lighting coming from low hanging bulbs and the dusty oblong tiffany lamps that hung over the pool tables. There was a small dance floor and I had a flashback to an uncomfortable time with Marlow, when I had been dancing with my then newly-minted boyfriend Tristan. Marlow had been playing a game of pool with Dakota, back before they were a couple. Tristan had been acting like an ass, treating me badly, and I'd felt embarrassed that Marlow had witnessed it.

Arriving between the lunch and supper crowd meant the place was only half full. We claimed a table along the back wall close to the bar.

A middle-aged woman with a salt-and-pepper French braid took our order. I'd been craving steak for a while now—probably low on iron or something—and got the steak sandwich. Marlow ordered a burger and fries. I was parched, so I was happy that our drinks arrived quickly. I took a long sip through the yellow, plastic straw. Marlow sat across from me, and ran a hand through his hair. It was shorter now, which I thought made him look older.

"Maybe Rudy Finch *is* our man," he said, "and accidentally killed himself."

"He was laid out pretty neatly," I said. "And stabbed."

"Yeah, I guess that would be hard to pull off," Marlow conceded.

"It's just so frustrating to be back to square one.

He's out there and we have no idea who he is." I stirred the ice in my drink, clinking it against the glass, soothed by the musical sound. "Are we sure it's even a he?"

"Yes. I saw him in the shed. Definitely a guy. Plus the security camera in the pawn shop proves it."

Our meals arrived and we slipped into easy conversation. This latest crime had bonded us again, like old times. We were there for each other—me for him, him for me. The dread I'd been living under since the accident had lifted and I felt hopeful and contented. We didn't have a suspect, but Marlow and I were a team again.

"How's the steak?" Marlow said.

I cut another piece, running it through the reddish brown juices and teased him with a low moan as I chewed. "Really yummy." It came out ad "mealy mummy," and he laughed. He reached out a fork playfully and I pulled my plate away from him. "Hey, stopped coveting my food."

"Get down!" Marlow yelled. In the split second while my mind was trying to register if he was kidding or serious, he shot out of his chair, threw himself into the seat beside me and flipped the table.

The blast of a gunshot was followed by screams and chaos as patrons scrambled for cover. Marlow covered me with his body, but in the mirror over the bar I could see the gunman. He wore a hockey mask.

"How—" I began, but Marlow hushed me. I trembled beneath his weight. It was too much of a coincidence for the masked man to choose to shoot up the same pub Marlow and I randomly chose to eat at. He was after us and he'd found us.

"M-M-Mar..." That stutter. I heard it before. It was the guy that Rudy Finch had been talking to in the hall. "M-M-M..." He switched to a sing-song voice. "Marlow Henry, stand up! Or I'll shoot at random."

Singing stopped his stutter.

The scene was majorly surreal.

I tugged on Marlow's arm, but couldn't stop him from slowly standing, arms raised in the air.

In the mirror I could see the masked man. He held his gun, arms stretched out. He was shaking so bad I was afraid he'd shoot Marlow by accident.

"Let's take this outside," Marlow said calmly.

"S-s-top!"

"It's me you want, right?" Marlow took a careful step forward. I knew he wanted to push the danger outdoors. He had a hero's heart, not even hesitating to risk his life. I really loved him in that moment.

I couldn't let the guy take Marlow. I stared at the knife in my hand. I had no memory of ever playing a throwing game, not even darts, but somehow I knew I knew how. My heart in my throat, I leaped up, exposing myself and hurled the steak knife through the air.

It landed in the middle of the man's chest. Not deeply—it wasn't that sharp of a knife, but enough to bite. He yelped and his knees buckled. On his way down he took a shot at Marlow, shattering the lamp above us instead. Marlow dove back behind the table with me. The room vibrated with terror-filled energy. We dropped to the ground flat on our stomachs. I pointed to the bar; we'd be more secure from a bullet there. We wormed toward it, inch by inch, my elbows feeling the burn from the carpet.

I kept my on eye on the masked man and stilled when he looked back at me. Pale blue eyes with dark pupils, narrowed and zeroing in on me. I froze with prickling fear. We wouldn't get behind the bar in time.

Just when I thought he'd point his gun and shoot, someone yelled, "Get him!"

The masked man disappeared before our very eyes.

Chapter Thirty-Eight

MARLOW

I HELPED SAGE UP. "Are you okay?"

"I'm fine." She brushed dust off her jeans as she stood. "Did you see what I saw?"

"Yep." Bedlam erupted in the room. Women crying, men shouting, some even running outside as if they might catch the gunman. I could see them through the open door looking up and down the street, knowing that they weren't going to find our culprit anywhere. Sirens screamed in the distance, growing louder as they drew closer.

I took Sage's hand and headed to the restrooms down a narrow hall behind the bar. I pulled her into the men's room with me, checked quickly that we were alone, and locked the door.

I whipped out my phone and dialed.

"Hey, Jack. I'm with Sage and I have you on speakerphone. There's been an incident at Harvey's pub. The masked man walked in pointing a gun."

"Any injuries?" Jack's voice remained professional, but I heard a tone of worry.

"The gun went off once. It killed a lampshade, but no one was hurt. Sage and I are okay, just a little shaken. He knows we're onto him, Jack. He called me out by name."

"Tell me exactly what happened."

I ran through the order of events, how Sage and I decided to stop for a bite to eat before heading back to campus, up to Sage's knife throw and the guy's disappearance.

"You're choice of eatery was impulsive?"

"Yes."

"He's tracking you somehow."

"Sage's truck?"

"Not possible. One of our guys inspected it before it was released to her." Made sense. Sage had only had her truck back for a couple of hours.

"The team's going to hack into the security camera at the pub to remove evidence of Sage's knife toss, good work, by the way—and the perp's disappearance. You guys should get out of there before the police arrive."

"We're on our way out now."

"And destroy your phones."

Sage threw me a look of horror. She said, "How will we contact you?"

"I'll have new phones delivered to your dorms later today."

Jack signed off and Sage and I slipped out the back door of the kitchen—I'd make sure to drop by later to settle the bill—and drove away just as the first cop car skidded into the pub's parking lot. I was glad Sage was driving because my nerves were shot and I couldn't keep my legs from bouncing. Sage's gaze darted to them but she didn't reach over to stop me.

"That was a close call," she said.

"Too close."

"The CISUE team is on it," she said. "Maybe we should take a step back and let them do their job."

I couldn't agree more. Not because some madman knew my name and probably wanted me dead, but because he'd seen me with Sage. I'd never forgive myself if something happened to her because of me. "Yeah, I think that's a good idea. I have a paper to write for tomorrow anyway."

Sage laughed. "Me too. Our lives are so crazy, Mars."

She dropped me off at my building and I held my palm out. "Give me your phone and I'll destroy it for you."

She handed it over. "How are you going to do that?"

"I can finally make good use of the dumbbells in the lounge."

She smiled and waved and I watched her go until her truck disappeared from view. I didn't even get inside when my phone buzzed again. Thinking it was Jack I whipped it out, but the text was from Dakota.

Dakota: Need to talk. Now.

Marlow: Your place or mine. :-)

Dakota: Be here in ten minutes.

An order. I'd been summoned. This couldn't be good.

I dashed inside to complete the kill-the-phones mission. It was surprisingly cathartic to destroy them.

"What the hell are you doing, man?" I jumped as Zed walked up behind me. "Have you lost your mind?"

"I'll explain later." I handed him the ruins. "Can you dump this for me?"

"What? I'm your garbage man now?"

I repeated, "I'll explain later."

Dakota knew it was a ten minute walk to her dorm from mine, and I'd already blown three. I had to jog now if I didn't want to make her even more angry than I could tell she was.

She was waiting outside when I got there, bundled up in her brown winter coat with a green scarf around her neck, a matching wool hat on her head with pink tufts of hair poking out. Her expression was bland—she didn't look happy or sad to see me. I predicted this was a bad sign.

"Marlow, this isn't working.""

"Dakota, I know a lot has been going on and I haven't been spending the time with you that I want to."

"No, please stop." She held out a hand and pressed it against my chest. "Let me speak."

"Okay."

"I really like you. I think you're a great guy and I enjoy hanging out with you. We had fun this summer, but I feel like there are three people in our relationship."

"Dakota..."

"Let me finish."

I let out a depressed sigh that manifested in the cold as a long puff of smoke.

"I know that Sage means more to you than you like me to believe."

"We're friends."

"I saw you drive by in her truck."

"What?"

"You were talking so intensely together you didn't even notice me on the sidewalk."

"Oh."

"You lied about having lunch with Jack, and you didn't take my calls because you were with *her*."

"I'm sorry I lied to you about Jack, but it's not what it looks like."

Dakota sighed. "Marlow, I think we'd be better off as friends."

In my mind I knew she was right. I hadn't been playing fair with her. My heart hadn't disengaged from Sage the way I had hoped. But honestly, I didn't know how Sage felt about me. She tended to blow hot and cold. Sometimes I thought from the way she looked at me that maybe she found me interesting or even attractive, and in the next moment she'd be cool and everything going on between us was strictly business.

Sage wasn't a factor at this moment. Not in the way Dakota imagined. With everything that had been happening with Jack and CISUE and the fact that I'd just been shot at—Dakota staying with me could actually be dangerous for her.

In the same way I had brought Sage into a dangerous situation today, I could just as easily put Dakota in harms way and not even realize it. For her safety's sake, she was right.

"I don't agree with you, at least not entirely, but if this is how you feel then I accept your decision. I just want you to know that I didn't come here expecting to break up. And even though I understand, I still feel kinda shocked."

Dakota reached out and patted my arm. "It'll be strange for a little while, but then us being just friends will feel normal again. And we'll be fine." She threw her arms around me in a quick hung, then disappeared into her building.

I walked away in a daze. Today I'd learned about CISUE, suffered through intense and awkwardly arousing defense moves with Sage, found a dead body, got shot at, and got dumped by my girlfriend.

Chapter Thirty-Nine

MARLOW HENRY always seemed to be with that pretty girl Sage Farrell even though the guy had a girlfriend. He hated guys like that—the kind who played around with women, who thought themselves as chick magnets and womanizers.

He wasn't that kind of guy. He would have been loyal to Crystal. He would never have cheated on her or flirted with other girls when she wasn't around. Crystal should have stayed true to him. He would've made her happy. He would've been good to her.

She deserved to die—he was glad it happened now.

Marlow Henry and the girl were having an intense conversation standing with only two feet between them. It irritated him that they were standing so close. He wished he knew what they were talking about.

He could easily teleport behind the brick pony

wall they stood next to, but he had no way of knowing what or who was on the other side of it, and he couldn't risk being spotted.

He had to be careful. Had to stay normal, not draw any unwanted attention to himself.

He wasn't sorry about what happened to Crystal anymore, or what he had done to Mr. Lambert. In fact, the desire to inflict harm on those who wronged him grew stronger every day. Like a massive sling shot pulling taut in his head, he wanted to let the stones of revenge go.

He had a list now of those who had to suffer. Marlow Henry was on it.

Chapter Forty

I MADE my way over to the student building for the last student government rally event. My eyes felt like sandpaper and I practically inhaled my coffee. With all the things that had been going on, plus papers to write and tests to study for, sleep eluded me. Like a stone skipping along the water, but just wouldn't sink.

I couldn't wait for this rally to be over as there was no chance now I was going to win seeing as half the student body thought me guilty of manslaughter and frowned at how unfair it was that I was walking about free while Crystal's life had ended.

Stella had upped her game. Helium balloons pinned to either side of her table were trying to float up to the ceiling and she dressed like she was running for Miss America instead of a government seat at DU.

"Look what the cat dragged in" she said with a smirk. "I have to give you chops for tenacity."

"I don't need anything from you, Stella."

Minji 's face reddened with embarrassment at her friend's behavior and I wondered why she hung around with Stella in the first place. I offered her a friendly smile, like we were comrades in the trenches here, and she surprised me by smiling back. Stella inserted herself into a small group of guys, flirting her way to a win. I shuffled over to Minji and asked, "Why do you hang out with her? She's really not nice to you."

"I don't know." Her dark eyes darted around the floor, too shy to look at me. "I've found it hard to make friends. She kind of took me under her wing."

I felt chastised. I'd spent the first month and a half of this semester feeling lonely and sorry for myself, not even thinking about others who might feel the same way. "We could hang out sometime," I said. She blinked a couple times and I wondered if maybe she drew the line at having friends accused of killing a person.

Her gaze finally settled on mine. "That would be nice."

I let out a breath. "Great. I just got a new phone. Let me put your number in."

When I glanced back up at Minji, I saw Stella behind her giving me a steely glare. "Minji," she called.

When Minji obediently responded, she handed her a couple bills. "Can you get me a diet Pepsi from the vending machine?"

I gave Stella a look of disapproval and she shot a haughty look back. I opened up my bag and removed the last stack of fliers. It wouldn't take me long to hand these babies out. I scanned the hall for a sign of Dakota, but couldn't see her pink hair anywhere. Instead I was surprised to see Marlow walking toward me.

"Where is Dakota?"

"I don't think she's coming today."

"Really? Is something wrong? Is she not feeling well?"

He stared out over my head. "We broke up last night."

I let out a soft "Oh."

"I hope I didn't have anything to do with it," I said gently. "I know I've been demanding a lot of your time lately."

"Not your fault. You didn't ask for these things to happen. And I can't tell Dakota the things I can tell you. Secrets in relationships just don't work. There are so many things I wanted to tell her that I couldn't and she could tell I was holding back." He let out a sigh. "I suppose it was only a matter of time."

"I'm sorry, Marlow. Must be painful."

"It is. I'll get over it."

I wasn't sure where to take the conversation from there and an awkward silence fell between us. I busied myself by spreading out the flyers into a nice fan shape on the table. Then I said, "Hey, before things get crazy here, do you mind watching the table for a minute? Nature calls."

"Sure. What do I do?"

"If someone approaches the table, hand them a flyer and kinda read out the points that state why they should vote for me." I shot him a faux-stern stare. "And look like you believe it."

He sent me a zealous look back; I wasn't sure if it was "faux" or not. "I do believe it," he said. "What does the flyer say anyway?" He held one up and made a show of squinting at it like he couldn't make it out.

"Ha ha," I said. I knew Marlow had the best vision on the planet, despite the glasses he often wore.

Just as I was pushing on the women's restroom door, I caught the sound of two guys talking, and heatedly. I peaked around the corner to see Wyatt arguing with Isaac.

"Stay away from her!"

"Cool down, man. We're just friends."

"Then stop being friends. She's my girlfriend." Wyatt shoved Isaac's shoulder. "Just keep your distance!"

"I can be friends with whoever I want. You're not

married to her. You don't own her." Isaac spun away toward the crowd leaving Wyatt to glare after him.

I headed into the restroom thinking that there was trouble in that corner. When I returned to the table, Marlow was busily talking with several people at once, and seemed like he was enjoying himself. Maybe he should be running for government. I didn't want to interrupt him and break the spell, so I waited until his conversation was over before joining him behind the table. "You're like a duck in water here."

"Don't be fooled. I hate talking to strangers."

"Well, good job at disguising that fact.""

He smiled crookedly down at me in the a way that made my knees feel weak. "I suppose it's part of my covert spy training."

Which reminded me of our connection to CISUE and the agreement Marlow and I had made. "I wonder when they'll call us in to wipe memories."

"Probably not until this case is solved."

Our attention was snagged by a commotion in the middle of the lobby. Screams echoed from the high ceiling as people scrambled behind the thick pillars or dropped to the floor.

Marlow grabbed my hand and yanked me down behind the table. "Not again," he groaned just as I spotted the source of the trouble.

Our hockey mask villain was back. He waved his

gun erratically, sparking more screams and sobs. Apparently he hadn't been injured too badly by the knife I'd thrown.

I whispered to Marlow, "What should we do?"

Before he could answer a gunshot was fired. Marlow took off like a track star.

"Marlow!" What did he think he was doing? He might be able to catch the guy, but this wasn't *The Matrix*. He couldn't dodge bullets.

I followed, but then stopped in my tracks. Blood. A body. People stunned to silence and staring.

Wyatt Banks lie dead in a pool of blood.

Stella's scream ripped through the eerie quiet. I searched the faces looking for his pal Isaac, but couldn't see him anywhere.

Chapter Forty-One

MARLOW

MAYHEM ERUPTED in the student building lobby. Near panic by some, and for others the opportunity to video the crime. I had no doubt that the incident had already been delivered to personal blogs and Facebook and Twitter feeds. I pushed through the crowds to get to Sage.

"Did you see him?" she asked.

"No. He's gone."

We stood shoulder to shoulder staring at Wyatt Bank's corpse.

"I saw him arguing with Isaac earlier," she said.

"Did you hear what they were arguing about?"

"Pretty sure it was about Stella. Wyatt didn't like how friendly Isaac and Stella were becoming."

Her statement made me think about Dakota and

how I knew she'd felt with Sage on the sidelines all the time.

"Where is Isaac now?" I asked.

Sage scanned the lobby. "I've tried to find him, but he's not here."

I tapped her elbow. "Let's go look for him."

We needed to leave quickly before the campus police arrived and held us back for questioning.

Wyatt and Isaac lived in the same dorm building as me. Sage and I hopped campus transit and got there in under five minutes. We hurried through the front door asking everyone we saw if they knew where Isaac Cavanaugh was. No one did.

News of the shooting had spread. The guys floating through the lounge area were tied to their phones, flipping through the DU news feeds.

"Wyatt Banks was just killed in the student building!"

"The shooter wore a hockey mask!"

"No one saw him leave, like, he vanished into thin air!"

Rob Hooper's bald-shaved head snapped up at the news. "Is that why you're asking for Isaac? He hasn't heard?"

"Yeah." I said. "Do you know where he is?"

Rob shook his head. "Sorry, man."

Sage followed me upstairs to the room on the

second floor that Isaac shared with Wyatt. I pounded on their door, but it was quiet on the other side and no one answered. "I don't think he's here."

"Where else could he be?"

"The library?" It was exam week.

"Let's go."

There was a soft buzz of murmuring amongst the students in the library. They weren't studying because they were all looking at their phones. We finally found Isaac at a table in the back, laptop open, headphones on. He seemed blissfully and conveniently unaware of the news everyone else was talking about.

I poked him in the shoulder and he jumped as if he was legitimately startled.

"You heard?"

Isaac slouched languidly. "Heard what?" His eyes moved from me to Sage. "Oh the lovely Sage is here. To what do I owe this pleasure?"

"Wyatt is dead," she said.

His gaze flickered from Sage to me, his stiff grin gradually fading. He was a convincing actor, but sociopaths often are.

"Are you joking?"

"No. I'm really sorry," Sage said.

Isaac's expression grew confused. "But I was just with him."

I noted how he didn't ask what happened. Though he appeared stunned, he didn't exactly seem grief-stricken.

Sage came to the same conclusion. "Aren't you going to ask us how he died?"

"Of course. I'm just so shocked. I can't believe Wyatt is gone. What happened?"

Sage proceeded to tell him about the shooting.

Isaac took his time to process this news. It was hard to tell if he was sincerely flabbergasted or planning his next move.

"That really sucks."

"Where were you, Isaac, twenty minutes ago?" Sage asked.

Isaac held a hand to his chest—a sign of offense, or protecting a tender stab wound?

"I've been right here for the last forty-five minutes. I didn't kill him. He was my friend."

"You don't look that upset about it," I said

"It hasn't really hit me yet. Everyone grieves in their own way. Now if you don't mind I'd like to get back to my studies." Isaac flipped his headphones back on his ears and tuned us out.

"What do you think of that?" I said in a near

whisper as we left him.

Sage twisted a strand of her dark hair around her slender finger, a move I found rather distracting.

"He's either a very good actor or mentally disturbed and completely lacks empathy."

I snapped back to attention. "He claims he wasn't there," I said. "And maybe he wasn't there as Isaac. He could've teleported in and out as the masked man."

"Most of the student body wasn't there," Sage said. "Every male student not in the lobby would have to be included as suspects."

"True."

"Say Isaac is our teleportation genius," Sage said. She leaned up against the bookshelves in the psychiatry section. "Maybe he's crazy enough to kill his friend over a tiff with a girl. But why would he kill Rudy?"

"Maybe Rudy did something to offend him. He wasn't the most amiable guy. I'm sure he'd offended most people that he'd encountered on campus."

"He was a jerk," Sage agreed. "I have to wonder why Professor Garvin hired him?"

"He was academically and intellectually qualified for the job," I said.

"Still doesn't give Isaac motive to kill Rudy."

"That we're aware of. And Isaac was besotted with Crystal Morrisette."

"How do you know that?" Sage asked

"I saw him..." I didn't want to reveal how the guys behaved when Wyatt was showing her latest picture around. "If Isaac is intelligent enough to develop a teleportation system, and if he wanted Crystal, maybe he used his technology to track her down and inserted himself in her life. She may have fought back, or maybe she played him, but whatever the case, his ego was wounded."

"So he killed her," Sage said.

"Maybe he just wanted to scare her."

"Then he got nervous and decided he needed a gun so he broke into the pawn shop to steal one," Sage said. "That was when he stole the old hockey mask."

"But what about the stutter?" I said. "Isaac didn't have any trouble talking just now."

Sage nodded slowly. "Maybe the stutter is an immediate after effect of teleportation and wears off."

We continued walking. "Whoever it is, his aggressive nature is accelerating. He's moved from maiming to stabbing to shooting," I said.

Sage poked me in the arm. "Don't forget he has his sights set on you. He must've figured out somehow that you were the one in his shed that night."

I watched Sage with a sense of regret and fear. I hated that she was pulled into these dangerous situations with me, but I felt helpless. I didn't know how to protect her.

"Are you all right, Marlow?"

Before I could answer we rounded the American history section and came across Zed and Dakota sitting at one of the dark wood library tables together. This wasn't an unusual situation since the three of us hung out quite a lot at the library and Zed and Dakota had become friends, but this time instead of sitting across the table from each other like they usually did, they sat closely on the same side.

I couldn't keep the irritation from my voice. "Don't you two look cozy?"

Zed jerked back, jaw dropping, but said nothing.

"Such a surprise to see you here with, Sage," Dakota snapped back. "Hi, Sage."

Sage's eyes darted to me with caution before responding. "Hey, guys."

Zed found his tongue. "Hey." He shifted his chair a couple inches back from Dakota. As if that would make a difference. He tried to diffuse the awkward situation by changing the topic. "Have you heard about the shooting in the student building?"

"We were both there," Sage said.

Dakota mumbled under her breath. "Of course you were."

"I was helping Sage with her campaign," I said tersely, "since you didn't show."

Dakota answered dryly, "So nice of you."

A slow simmering anger boiled in my stomach as we left the library. But strangely, I wasn't mad at Dakota. I was mad at Zed.

Chapter Forty-Two

SAGE

BY THE TIME we left the library the whole campus was on lockdown. Security sealed all of the exits and the police had cruisers stationed there to question anyone trying to get in or out. Every person known to have been in the student building was required to give a statement to the police. I had the unfortunate luck of being interviewed by Detective Landsky.

"You again?" he said, mustache twitching. "How is it that I always find you in the middle of everything?"

"It was purely coincidental that I was here," I said. "I'm running for a student government seat and today was the last rally to encourage students to come and vote. That's why there were more than the usual number in attendance. The hall isn't normally this busy at this time of day."

"I see. Miss Farrell, are you in possession of a Smith & Wesson 9mm Shield?"

"No, sir. I don't own any guns."

"That wasn't what I asked. Are you in possession of a Smith & Wesson 9mm Shield?"

"No."

He studied me with his beady eyes. "You realize that you are still under investigation for the death of Crystal Morrisette right? The fact that you are out on bail does not equate to an acquittal."

So much had happened since the night of the bush party, by now the whole event felt like a rumor about someone else and not an awful accident that happened to me.

"Yes, sir."

He petted his mustache and I had to wonder if there was a woman in his life, and if so, why she hadn't insisted he shave the damn thing off.

"Do you have anything to add?" he asked.

I huffed. "Obviously I didn't kill Wyatt Banks because I was in the room with the shooter."

"I understand that, but we haven't ruled out the possibility that the shooter might have an accomplice. The security footage from the incident at Harvey's Pub shows that you were there too and for some inexplicable reason you fled the scene without giving your statement." He looked at me with disapproval. "So you see what I'm saying, right?"

I could only nod.

"We still don't know what happened there exactly, except that we have a witness that said a woman threw a knife, causing the shooter to drop to the ground. That was the last they saw of both the woman and the shooter."

"If I was working with the shooter, why would I throw a knife at him?" I said snidely. "Hypothetically?"

"You tell me."

"I wouldn't. Besides, the first incident was an accident," I said. "Do you have any evidence other than circumstantial to connect me to any of these crimes, Detective?"

The little animal above Landsky's lips quivered. He leaned back in his chair and let out a belch. "Thank you for your time, Miss Farrell. We'll be in touch. Don't leave town."

Over the next couple of days Marlow and I did what we could to keep an eye on Isaac Cavanaugh. He was in some of Marlow's classes, which helped with that, but I took more of a stealth approach. Staying close to him by picking a table near him in the dining hall, for example. Not so surprisingly, Stella and Minji sat with him. To comfort each other over Wyatt's death, I supposed.

I chose a table in the library to study in the same section as him. I didn't know what I hoped to discover. I followed him into the Literary Café, taking a table across the room. I wore my purple frame glasses just for a different look. People get used to a person's face with or without glasses and changing it up can throw them off. I watched Isaac from the corner of my eye while I did some research for a biology project. Isaac stood and I worried he was going to leave, but he only went to use the restroom. I shielded my face with a textbook when he walked by.

I should have given Isaac more credit. He startled me by noisily pulling out the empty chair next to me, then cocked his head and leaned in. "Why are you following me?"

Damn. I needed to get on the CISUE team to get them to teach me how to do a better job of trailing a person. I obviously sucked at it. I decided to play coy. "What makes you think I'm following you? I'm a student here too. We're bound to be in the same places at the same time on occasion."

"You know what I think?"

That you're guilty of murder?

"I think you have a thing for me."

My mouth dropped open. Conceited jerk! "I do not. It's just a coincidence."

"A coincidence is when your friend gets shot just after you've left the room. And then because of that coincidence, everyone assumes that you must've killed him because you weren't by his side at his moment of need."

"Sorry if I offended you by my questions," I said carefully. "It was unfair. I was just shaken up after watching someone get shot only feet away from me."

Isaac's expression softened. "I see. That would be traumatic. Can we start over? Would you like to go out sometime?"

I couldn't help but laugh. "Should we invite Stella along?"

The lines on his forehead deepened. "Why would you say that?"

"Just that... you seem... close."

"I'm just being a friend to her. She's grieving. But it's you I like, Sage."

I got goose bumps and I wasn't sure if it was because we shared a romantic chemistry or if it was because I was being hit on by a killer.

"So?" he prompted.

"I don't know."

He was charming and, I had to admit, good-looking. Going on a date with Isaac could be a good under cover gig. It would give me a chance to work on my spy skills.

Oh, man. Why was I always attracted to bad boys?

No. I'd learned my lesson. I didn't go for guys like that anymore. I went for guys like Marlow. No pretenses or false flattery. No hidden agendas. What you saw was what you got. Hopefully someday Marlow would decide that he went for girls like me too. In the meantime, it wouldn't hurt to go out with Isaac and see what I could find out.

"Come on, Sage. Nothing serious. Just dinner."

I took off my glasses and flashed a flirtatious smile. Tilting my chin down, I stared at him from under my eyelashes. "Okay. Where do you want to go?"

"Well, for a first date we should keep it casual." He grinned. "We're already sitting here having coffee so we can scratch that off the list of relationship must-dos."

I sipped my coffee and nodded in agreement.

"How about pizza?"

"Pizza Haven?"

"Sure. Tomorrow at seven?"

"Okay. I'll meet you there."

"That's great," he said. "I look forward to it."

He cast a sly look over his shoulder as he left. "Do keep stalking me in the meantime."

Chapter Forty-Three

MARLOW

ZED'S FEET were always cold so he'd bought a small space heater and had it plugged on his side of the room. Usually I appreciated the extra warmth, especially this time of year, but despite the factual room temperature the small space between us was frosty.

I couldn't remember the last time Zed and I had fought. Maybe it was the winter when we were ten and I hit him square in the face with a snow ball. I hadn't been able to stop laughing, but apparently it had been more of an ice ball and Zed had ended up with a black eye.

Zed studiously ignored me and I pretended to read my textbook, though the words just swirled around the page meaninglessly as my mind refused to focus. I tortured myself by reliving the scene in the library, how Zed had so quickly claimed my seat beside Dakota and how chummy they'd looked.

The pressure in my chest built to the boiling point. "You sure didn't waste any time!"

Zed didn't bother to look up. "Neither did you."

"What?"

"You're mad that I'm making a move on Dakota, but you have a big freakin' log in your eye."

"What the hell are you talking about?"

His book dropped to his lap and he stared across the narrow gap between our beds at me. "It's from the Bible, about pointing out a splinter in someone else's eye when you got a big log in your own. You're judging me for something that you are doing and have been doing for months: pining for Sage."

"Have you been *pining* for my girlfriend all these months?"

"Ex-girlfriend. Dakota and I are friends. We hang out a lot. You probably didn't notice because you're always off with S*age*."

I hated the way he say *Dakota and I*.

"But, couldn't you even wait a day? We just broke up!"

"*You* didn't wait a day, did you? If I do say so myself, and I *do* say so, you were a lousy boyfriend."

I wanted to throw my heavy textbook at his hairy mug, but instead I grabbed my jacket and slammed the door on my way out.

The wind slapped my face, and I thrust my chin out for more abuse. By the time I'd made it across the park behind the library, the flame of my self-righteous indignation had fizzled into embers of self-loathing.

Zed was right. I did have a big freakin' log in my eye. Without Dakota around it was impossible to keep denying the truth: I was in love with Sage.

Admitting this fact to myself somehow conjured her up.

"Marlow!"

She was like a mirage, haloed in the low-angle rays of the setting sun, like a beautiful brunette angel. I wanted to reach out and touch her, needing to know if she was real or if I had crossed over into teleportation-induced insanity.

"Marlow? Are you okay?"

She stepped toward me, into the shadow of a red oak tree, and the ethereal effect disappeared. My throat felt dry and I found it hard to swallow.

"Yeah, uh, I'm fine."

"Are you sure? You look upset."

"No, just, Zed was being an ass so I left."

"Isaac just asked me out."

"What? W-why?" I stammered.

"Why did he ask me out?" Sage looked offended. "Some guys are attracted to me."

"No, of course they are. That's not what I meant."

"What did you mean?"

"Nothing. You told him no, right?"

"No."

"You said yes? Are you crazy?"

"No I'm not crazy, Mars. This is a perfect chance to get close to our suspect. Maybe he'll give up some info that could tie him to this case. Reveal evidence of his guilt."

"Are you hearing yourself? You want to go out with a potential serial killer! It's too dangerous."

"We're just going to Pizza Haven. It's public, lots of people there."

"We don't know how his system works. Maybe all he has to do is touch you to take you with him. And zap, and you're gone from the restaurant to who knows where."

"I'll be careful. I won't let him get close enough to touch me. We'll sit at one of those big booths."

I shook my head. "No. You're not doing it."

She squinted her gorgeous brown eyes, scowled at me. "You're not the boss of me, Marlow Henry. I'm a grown woman. I can do what I want."

"Even if it's stupid?"

"Yes! Even if it's stupid."

She stormed off. And all I could think about was how beautiful she was when she was mad.

Chapter Forty-Four

HE DIDN'T KNOW why he hadn't thought of it sooner, with so many abandoned homes in the Detroit area. He found one not far from the university, isolated at the end of a weed-covered cul-de-sac. Over the years the wind had torn off the roof making the one-story house unappealing to squatters. But it had a cellar with a heavy door that kept out the rain. Wooden stairs with loose boards led to the damp room that stank of mold and rotting potatoes. There were a couple small windows tucked up against the ceiling filled with cobwebs and dead bugs and shedding insufficient light.

No working utilities meant he had to set up a generator to run his equipment. A Coleman camping lantern brightened the room, and at least he could get a Wi-Fi signal, thanks to an open connection in the neighborhood.

He preferred solitude, and after a while he didn't even notice the smell. His focus was lasered on the Facebook page belonging to Sage Farrell. Her photo albums pleased him. She had deep brown eyes, the most beautiful, provocative soul-searching eyes he'd ever seen. She was gorgeous and intelligent—look at all the activities that she was involved in! She wasn't a tramp like Crystal. Sage was loyal and loving. Honest and pure.

Hacking skills used to be something unique; people sought you out to do the "impossible" if you had them. Now they were almost commonplace. It surprised him that a guy as smart as Marlow Henry would think changing phones would put him off scent.

He had access to Marlow Henry's phone, and therefore he had access to Marlow Henry's life.

This cat and mouse game would be over soon, and the lovely Sage Farrell would be his.

Chapter Forty-Five

SAGE

I ARRIVED at Pizza Haven early because I wanted to be the one to decide where Isaac and I sat. There was a booth with red vinyl seats near the door and I slid onto the bench closest to it staying on the outside edge to prevent Isaac from squeezing in beside me. I kept my coat and gloves on, not exactly sure if that would help me if Isaac just grabbed at me to teleport. I hadn't really thought this through. Did he have to touch me skin to skin or just be holding onto me somehow? I started to feel uneasy knowing I was here alone and wondered if maybe Marlow's ominous prediction that I was on an ill-fated venture was right.

A female server dressed in a short black skirt asked if I was waiting for someone and gave me two menus when I said yes. I ordered a hot tea.

I surveyed the room, memorizing the details—I was on spy duty after all. Eight booths, four along the window, four along the back wall, six tables in the center set for four. Three of the booths and two of the tables had customers. Large impressionist prints of Italy hung on the walls. There was a framed picture of the Italian family who ran the restaurant hung near the kitchen along with a fire alarm box.

I felt the blast of cool air as the door opened. I twisted to smile at Isaac fully expecting him to scoot into the seat in front of me. But it wasn't Isaac—it was Marlow. "What are you doing here?" I whispered angrily.

He stuffed his hands deep into his coat pockets and shrugged. "I'm hungry."

He slid into an empty booth along the wall, choosing the seat that faced me. Part of me fumed at Marlow's lack of confidence in me, but a bigger part was actually really glad to have him here.

The time on my phone was 7:12. Isaac was twelve minutes late. I snorted nervously, wondering if I was being stood up. The door opened again and this time it was Isaac. I waved at him and pointed to the seat in front of me keeping eye contact so that he wouldn't be tempted to look around and possibly spot Marlow staring.

My tea arrived just after Isaac did and I held onto

it. If he made a move, I was going to splash him in the face.

"So good to see you again, Sage," he said with a considerable dose of charm. "You look great."

I put on a flirty smile and giggled. "Thanks. You don't look so bad yourself."

Our server came back and asked if we were ready to order. I hadn't even had a chance to open the menu, but Isaac had obviously been here before and already knew what he wanted. "Is it okay if I order for both of us?"

Sure, why not? I nodded.

"Is there anything you don't like?"

"I like everything."

He ordered a large half meat lovers half vegetarian with extra cheese and a bottle of red wine. "That way we have all the food groups," he said. "Meat, vegetables, grain, dairy and fruit. Pretty smart, huh?"

The "fruit" arrived first and the server poured us each a glass. Isaac held his up for me to toast. "To a new day and new friendships."

I clanked his glass and giggled again. "Nothing cliché about that."

He stared at me over the top of his glass. "Why don't you tell me about yourself."

"What do you already know?"

He hummed. "You want to make a difference,

which is why you're running for a seat on the student council. You're intelligent and like to hang out with intelligent people even if they're nerds and geeks."

I forced myself to keep my eyes on Isaac and not let my gaze flitter over to "one particular geek" whom I could see from my peripheral vision was scowling at me.

"That's more than I know about you," I lied. "Why don't you start?"

"Okay. My father's a hospital administrator and my mother's a sitting Judge, the Honorable Esme Cavanaugh."

"Wow. How was that growing up?"

"The woman has keen senses." He smirked. "I couldn't get away with much."

The way his eyes twinkled, I doubted that. I suspected his mother had been too busy dealing with the district's delinquents that she hardly had time to notice the one right under her nose.

"Why'd you choose to study at DU?" I asked. Isaac had enough smarts and his family enough money to have had his pick of Ivy League colleges.

"I heard this is where the pretty girls go."

I fluttered my eyelashes as if I appreciated the blatant flattery. "I'm sure there are pretty girls everywhere."

"That's true and part of the problem." His gaze fell

to his hands and he twisted his wine glass as he spoke. "I got into a situation... with a girl... the case was dropped, but those schools got wind of it."

Was he saying he had raped someone? It triggered the pain of losing Teagan who suffered terribly that way and died.

He watched me intently waiting for my reaction, and I wondered if he got some twisted thrill out of saying shocking things to people. I worked to keep a neutral expression not wanting to give him the satisfaction. I had to remind myself I was on a job and not a real date.

"Well, lucky for you then, that you are free to attend here. Speaking of pretty girls, how's Stella?"

His chin jutted up in surprise—whether at the sudden change of topic, or that the new topic was Stella, I wasn't sure.

"Stella has highs and lows," he finally said. "Her relationship with Wyatt was... challenging, but his death is still a shock."

"I heard Wyatt was the jealous type. That you guys argued over Stella."

Isaac jerked. "Where did you hear that?"

"Well, maybe I didn't hear it. I sensed it."

"Sensed it?"

"Yes, when you were both with Stella in the student building."

243

"Ah. So I can add perceptiveness to your list of traits?"

"I suppose."

"Anyway, it doesn't matter now. He's dead and Stella's free."

The way he said that so flatly sent chills up my spine.

I made sure not to lean in, and to keep my hands and elbows off the table. I even tucked my feet under the seat. In no way did I want Isaac to touch me.

"I, uh, need to visit the rest—"

Isaac's head spun, his eyes pinned on something over my shoulder, and his face blanched as if he'd just seen a ghost.

I turned to see what he was looking at. Everything seemed to slow down.

The skull mask stared at me.

I screamed.

My tea spilled.

I ducked underneath the table as far as I could, almost hugging Isaac's legs.

There was a shrill ringing sound and water sprouted from the ceiling.

People wailed and swore.

Droplets spilled over the edge of the table onto my head.

"Sage?"

It was Marlow's voice. Shaking with relief, I reached for his hand and he helped me out of the booth.

"You pulled the fire alarm?" I said.

He nodded. "The masked man disappeared. Not sure how his system works if it's wet."

I looked around the restaurant for Isaac.

"He's gone too."

"Not surprising," I said. "I didn't peg him as the chivalrous type."

"Nope," Marlow said. "We should get out of here before the fire truck arrives." He dropped a bunch of bills on the table to cover my uneaten meal.

I sighed. Isaac Cavanaugh might be a jerk, but he was officially off our suspect list. We were back to square one.

Chapter Forty-Six

MARLOW

I HADN'T SLEPT WELL since the date incident with Isaac Cavanaugh who turned out not to be the real danger. What stirred the cold fear in my belly was the fact that the unknown masked man hadn't come for me, but for *Sage*.

Why did he want her? How did he even know about her? It must've been me. He'd seen her with me and now she was in danger. I could barely stand myself for being responsible for putting Sage in this perilous situation.

I became so manic about calling and texting her to make sure she was all right, hovering like her shadow when we were in the same room, that she actually told me to give her some space. If I'd hoped to win her over, I was losing ground on that front.

So I was pleasantly surprised to see Sage's name when my phone buzzed.

Sage: Marlow, can you please meet me at the park bench outside the student building? I've got news.

Marlow: When?

Sage: Now. It's important.

My pulse quickened. I was tempted to text her back and ask for details, but if Sage felt it would be safe to do that she would have. Whatever information she'd gained was sensitive enough that she wanted to tell me in person. Thankfully I had forty minutes before my next class so there was time to head over to the park behind the student building.

The park had no name as it was generally considered part of the campus grounds, and due to a lack of funds, grounds keeping had become low priority, which resulted in untrimmed bushes and hedges that grew wildly. Eventually a section of brush expanded around a lone rusty bench, like a horseshoe, and a lot of the student population didn't even know the small alcove existed. Sage had discovered it with her work running for student council and had told me about it.

From the urgency of Sage's text I had expected her to be there already, but the bench was empty. I lowered myself onto it, planted my elbows on my knees and waited. A couple minutes later the bushes moved aggressively, opposing the direction of the wind, as if something was attempting to walk through it.

I'd expected Sage to materialize and blinked as my mind registered that the person standing before me wasn't Sage but the masked man. A new kind of fear gripped me.

Jumping to my feet, I half-stumbled over the bench. "Hold on, man!" I said, not wanting to give the guy a chance to reach for me. My eyes darted around and behind him, searching for Sage ready to warn her.

"Sh-she's not coming, g-genius. The t-text you got was from m-me."

I was stunned. "You hacked my phone?" I really thought I'd put every safe-guard on it.

"It wasn't hard."

He took a step forward and I took a step back. "What do you want?"

"I w-want c-credit!"

"You'll have it," I said. "Once we know who you are."

He flipped his mask to the top of his head, revealing his pug-nosed face.

"Harland?"

He grinned at me like the cat who'd caught the mouse, ready to play a little before making the final kill. "Hiding in p-plain sight this whole t-time."

"But, I don't get it. Why'd you kill Crystal Morrisette?"

"I didn't. Sage F-Farrell did that."

"You teleported her in front of Sage's truck."

"I had no way of k-knowing exactly when S-Sage, or anyone for that matter, would be d-driving on that road. I thought everyone would b-be at the p-party. I only meant t-to t-teach her a lesson."

"What lesson would that be?"

"Not t-to b-betray me! She was a ch-cheater and a liar. Wanted to m-make a b-big appearance at the p-party to b-boost her career. I thought a long w-walk would show her who's b-boss."

"What about Rudy Finch?"

"He gave me an unfair g-grade. He was j-jealous. My p-paper was eons b-better than anything he's ever wr-written."

It was possible that was true, but Rudy hadn't deserved to die for it.

"And Wyatt Banks?"

"He made f-fun of me."

"That's it? You killed him for that?"

"I've been t-teased and p-picked on my whole life! I'm b-better than him, b-better than all of you!"

Harland hadn't produced a weapon, he was only armed with his teleportation device. I supposed he didn't want to draw attention by killing me here with a gun, or chance that a stab wound might not do the job.

He had picked this place strategically. He stood between me and my exit. There was no way I could pass him without giving him an opportunity to grab me.

"What did I ever do to you?" I asked.

"You d-discovered my s-secret. My p-project. You st-stole my b-big moment. I wanted to sh-showcase it to the w-world at the New S-Scientist Innovation Award c-contest. They t-televise that now, you know? And with s-social m-media? Everyone w-would've heard about me. They'd remember my f-face and my n-name. I would've b-been s-someone!"

I knew if I let him touch me I'd be dead.

Chapter Forty-Seven

SAGE

THE WEATHER HAD TURNED UNUSUALLY WARM AGAIN, so today felt more like an early spring day than late fall. Instead of speed-walking from class to class to escape the cold, students strolled casually and mingled about, like someone had turned the dial to slow-motion.

I'd over-dressed, feeling hot under my winter coat and accessories, and removed my sky blue wool scarf and hat. I stuffed them into my bag as I shuffled through a mound of dry brown leaves, not paying attention to where I was going and accidentally bumped into someone.

It was a shock to see Dakota's face. "Oh, sorry!" I almost didn't recognize her because her pink hair was now blue.

"It's fine." She seemed surprised as well.

"Your hair," I said. "I like it."

"Thanks." She pushed a strand of blue behind her ears. "It was time for a change."

I got the double meaning.

"I'm sorry to hear about you and Marlow."

She cocked her head and raised a blond brow. "Are you really?"

We stared at each other for a painful moment. We both knew the truth, and lying would just add insult to injury.

"I am sorry that you've been hurt."

Dakota shrugged and kicked at the leaves. "I'm okay, actually." She looked up again. "And I'm okay if you and Marlow are together."

"We're not."

"It's a matter of time, I suspect. But, I'm fine, really. Marlow always had eyes for you. Besides Zed and I are just a better fit."

"It's official then?"

"We're going slow, but yeah."

It was such a relief to hear it. A genuine smile claimed my face. "I'm happy for you. You guys make a cute couple."

My phone rang and a quick look showed Jack's name. Strange. He usually called Marlow.

"I have to take this."

Dakota waved me off. "Sure, I'm meeting Zed at Java Junkie anyway."

I glanced across the street in time to see Zed arriving at the coffee shop and waved before answering. "Jack?"

"Are you with Marlow?" His voice was tense and made me nervous.

"No, why?"

"He's not responding to my calls. We got the analysis back on the paint chip. It was the kind used to paint images onto old hockey masks from the '70s."

"That ties the masked man to Rudy's death."

"Yes. A hockey mask was stolen from the pawn shop. We showed the owner photos of every male science student currently attending or recently graduated from DU. He identified the man as Harland Payne."

I gasped. "He's one of the science geeks that hangs out with Marlow!"

"Marlow's cell is pinging from behind the student building."

"There's a small park there."

"Sage, I want you to stay where you are. My team and I are on our way."

"But I'm right here!"

"It's too dangerous."

He clicked off and I shook my head, astounded. All

that clandestine training, and he wanted me to sit on my hands while Marlow might be in trouble? Hell, no.

It took me about ten minutes to get from Java Junkie to the student building. I circled around the bushes and hedges that made the small park a haven for young lovers looking for a bit of privacy. It was also known for more nefarious activities involving the drug trade. I ducked low and peeked through the brush.

Harland had Marlow trapped in the narrow end of the alcove. They were talking, but I couldn't hear what they were saying. Marlow was likely trying to talk sense into him, but I knew that Harland was beyond reasoning. My pulse raced. There was no way Marlow could dodge Harland without brushing against him. Harland was inching closer and I knew he intended to take Marlow. Before I even knew what I was doing I picked up a stone, stepped out from behind the brush, and threw it expertly, hitting Harland square in the head.

Harland yelled out, grabbed the back of his skull and dropped to his knees. Marlow tried to deke past, but Harland's hand shot out and clasped Marlow's ankle, bringing him down.

I gasped, half expecting them to disappear before my eyes, but then I noticed Harland's free hand was empty.

I pounced on Harland. He yelped but let go of

Marlow. Marlow jumped to his feet, just as Harland latched onto me. Harland held up his other arm. "I have it!"

The teleporter device was in his hand.

Marlow's eyes filled with fear and he shouted, "No! It's me you want. Take me!"

"I want b-both of you!"

I jabbed my elbow into Harland's ribs hard, figuring I didn't have anything to lose. Marlow sprang between us, securing my freedom.

Then he disappeared before my eyes.

"Marlow!"

I buckled over, unable to breathe. Harland Payne was a cold-blooded murderer. Marlow was as good as dead. A sob escaped my lips.

Chapter Forty-Eight

MARLOW

I COULDN'T LET Harland teleport with Sage. Not that I thought he'd kill her—I believed he wanted to make her his new Crystal—but to save her soul. No one knew what really happened to a person on a spiritual or energy level after every single cell was disassembled. It was already too late for me. I jumped between Sage and Harland, effectively breaking his hold on her. I heard the sound of her screaming, then it suddenly cut to quiet.

Awareness dawned slowly. The air smelt dank and musty. I squinted upward to narrow windows tucked in close to the ceiling, dirty and covered in cobwebs, letting in just enough light to illuminate a swirl of dust particles. I was tapped to a chair, trussed up like a turkey.

I didn't know how much time had passed. Ten minutes? An hour? More? The nerves in my wrists and ankles tingled from lack of circulation. My back clenched with stiffness, and the chloroform Harland had knocked me out with had given me a hell of a headache. To make it worse, my mouth was sealed with duct tape and the dust irritated my nose.

How did I always manage to get into these kinds of situations?

I pinched my eyes closed and willed the tickle to go away to no avail. The sneeze let go through my nostrils and my cranium exploded.

I moaned as pain knocked about between my ears.

Harland, dressed in all black, had the hockey mask pushed up on the top of his head. I wondered why he bothered wearing it, even half-way, at all. He sat huddled over a keyboard on a makeshift desk, and I recognized the stack of equipment that I now had the deepest respect for.

My ankles were secured to an old wooden chair, probably as old as this cellar, but that didn't stop my knees from jumping. Not only was my future not too bright, but I'd teleported for the second time. Twice dead. Was I on my way to crazydom like Harland

Payne? At what point would the stutter kick in. Maybe it had already. I just hadn't had a chance to test my voice out yet.

Harland faced me and motioned to his equipment. "It's a b-beaut, h-hey?"

I nodded.

"I b-b-bet you w-wish you inv-v-v-v..."

Harland's features twisted in frustration. He shouted in song, "INVENTED IT!"

His eyes were wide and wild and flickered around the cellar and I doubted I had much time. The chair I was tied to was in the middle of the room—nothing behind me to rub the tape against to saw through it. Moving my hands in an effort to tear it just seemed to make the lack of circulation worse.

Harland paced, pulling the mask back over his face. If it weren't for his stutter, he'd probably be telling me how he discovered the key to teleportation, how the equipment worked. Bragging to someone who could understand what he was talking about would be so satisfying. This probably wasn't how he'd pictured the preamble before killing me would go down. I worried he'd take his frustrations out on me, maybe with his fists or a loose board, but he raced up the steps instead, leaving me alone.

I felt helpless. There had to be something I could do to get out of this fix. *Think Henry, think!*

As best I could I shuffled toward the desk. Maybe Harland was in possession of a pair of scissors, or maybe I could figure out how to teleport myself out of here. The handheld device sat on the desk, drawing my eye like a beacon.

Putting any kind of weight on my feet made me cry out in pain, a zillion fire ants biting every square inch of my feet and up my calves. My nose was dry and burned from breathing so hard through it. I was afraid it was going to start bleeding.

All my efforts only bought me inches. The light in the room dimmed to darkness in the meantime. My throat was so dry that I felt dizzy from dehydration.

How did I get in this situation? I trusted a phone text from Sage. I should've known it wasn't her. Now that I thought about it, it wasn't the way she talked. It was too formal. She would've called me Mars and never would've said please. If I was going to protect her, I had to up my game. I had to engage my senses, I had to pay attention.

Oh no. My chest squeezed at a dark thought. Was that where Harland had gone? Had he gone after Sage?

It was dark, but I could see well enough to judge that the distance between me and the device was about six feet. It might as well be six miles. I kept Sage's face in my mind as I pushed through the pain. The space grew shorter—five feet, four feet, three. Almost there. But then what?

The bulb suddenly lit, its brightness blinding me, and Harland's footsteps thumped down the stairs.

He had a bottle of water and drank it flauntingly. He wiped his mouth. "I n-n-needed to th-think."

At least Sage wasn't with him. I grunted, pointing my chin to his bottle, begging with my eyes for a drink.

He smirked and set the bottle down on the desk beside the device. He stared at the drag marks on the dirt floor. "G-going s-s-somewhere?" Then he sat down and woke up his monitor, turning it toward me so I could see it.

He brought up a blank word processor document and typed:

You stole my glory. You stole my fame. You stole my future. Now I'm going to steal from you.

Sage's beautiful face filled the screen. "M—m-mine."

"No!" It was a useless, wordless sound, but it made Harland laugh.

He typed again:

I have the co-ordinates for her bed in her dorm room. I will go to her tonight while she's sleeping and take her. There is nothing you can do about it.

He stared at me, the expression on his face clearly

saying that he thought himself the victor. I huffed and puffed, but couldn't blow his house down.

More typing:

How does it feel? To be helpless and alone? IT SUCKS, RIGHT? I WILL HAVE SAGE AND YOU WILL DIE.

Harland reached into his pocket and produced a jack knife. I jerked back, impulsively keeping my chin down to protect my neck.

Suddenly there was a crash and the thunder of boots on the steps. "Drop that knife!" a voice yelled. A SWAT team in heavy black vests burst into the cellar, taut arms stretched out front, guns pointed. The first man was Jack.

Harland sprung behind me, snapped my head back and held the knife to my throat.

"S-stay back!"

Jack partially lowered his gun. "Calm down, Harland. We don't want to hurt you."

"S-s-tay b-b-back! I'll k-kill him."

Staring up over my head I could see the crazed look in Harland's eyes. If he killed me, he'd be shot on the spot. I didn't think Harland wanted to die just yet. His eyes darted to the handheld device on the desk. He loosened his grip on me and dashed for it.

I threw all my weight sideways against my bonds. The chair tipped with me, crashing against the desk.

As the chair and I hit the floor, the device went flying. Harland dove for it, knocking over the stack of equipment; the edge of the monitor came down on my ankle, white-hot pain shot stars across my vision, and I screamed.

"We got him!" someone said. Agent Black had Harland Payne on the ground, facedown, nose pushed into the dirty floorboards.

Jack rushed to me, carefully peeled the tape from my mouth, cut the tape from my ankles and wrists and helped me get upright again. I yelped as the blood returned to extremities.

"Nice move," he said.

"Easy on my ankle," I grunted.

"Marlow!"

I twisted toward Sage's voice and I smiled through the pain. "Hey. Nice to see you."

Harland was taken away and a couple medics looked at my ankle, which was throbbing fiercely. They figured it was broken. Awesome. They brought down a stretcher and lifted me on it. With Sage there I tried to act tough, but it hurt like a son of a bitch.

"Good work you guys," Jack said to Sage and me.

"Sage, I'll make sure your name is cleared of all charges and that everyone knows that you had a hand in helping to catch the killer."

Sage and I shared a look of relief and satisfaction. We were a good team.

"But now it's time to go back to CISUE," Jack said. "Our doctors will set your leg, Marlow, and then we need to complete the terms of our agreement."

"You're serious about erasing our memories?" Sage said. "Will we forget everything?"

"You'll remember the basics, but no details. You won't remember CISUE or anyone you met there."

"Even you?"

"You'll remember me, but only as Marlow's dad."

Sage conceded though I could tell by the long sigh and the slump of her shoulders that she was doing it reluctantly. The medics lifted me up the stairs on the stretcher. Images of me sliding off and onto my back on the cellar floor crossed my mind as the angle sharpened, and I was glad I'd been strapped down.

Chapter Forty-Nine

SAGE

MARLOW SAT PROPPED up against his pillow, his long legs stretched out in front of him, one sock hanging loose from a narrow foot and the other encased in a clunky stocking of plaster. His side of the room was marginally cleaner than Zed's, which almost matched Nora's F5-category tornado preference.

I knew Zed wouldn't be here because I'd seen him walking through campus with Dakota on his arm. It was an impulsive decision to come.

My heart did backflips as I stood there, alternately accusing me of being an idiot for risking a valued friendship by speaking the truth out loud and congratulating me for finally having the courage to do it.

I'd surprised him by coming unannounced. "This

has been a sucky week for you," I said. "Broken ankle, broken heart."

Marlow shifted upright as if to give me his full attention. "I'm not really that heart-broken."

My gaze locked onto his emerald eyes, so gorgeous to me now. I didn't want him to wear lenses ever again. "What do you mean?" I needed to know, before I said anything humiliating I couldn't unsay. I watched Marlow's expression closely for any sign that he was still in love with Dakota.

He swallowed and said the words that made my heart hope. "She wasn't the girl for me."

"Then, who is the girl for you?" My voice was breathy, like I'd just run onto a suspension bridge swinging precariously underneath me. A weighted silence hung between us. My heart beat noisily against my ribs. The next thing Marlow said could change everything. I'd make it safely off the bridge to the other side or I'd fall.

"You?"

He said it so softly I almost didn't hear it. "What?"

"You." This time he said it boldly, with confidence. "If it's what you want."

I felt a corny smile spread across my face. "I do want."

Marlow hooted and fist bumped the air. "Yes! There is a God!"

I laughed out loud, feeling warm with relief. Marlow always knew how to make me laugh. He wanted me, I wanted him. It was finally out in the open. "So what do we do now?"

The corner of Marlow's mouth curved up into a goofy grin. "I don't know. This is new territory for me."

"For me too," I said with a wink. "I guess we'll have to explore it together."

He shifted toward the wall and patted the free space beside him. I could barely breathe as I stepped toward him, and sat, the bed sinking under my weight, pushing us closer. He threaded his fingers through mine and studied our entwined hands. His touch was so familiar to me from all the times he'd clutched my hands when we had to run for our lives, but this felt really different.

"We have been known for our adventures," Marlow said. "I'm ready to explore if you are." He pulled me closer until our foreheads touched. My lips tickled his as I whispered, "I'm ready, Marlow Henry. I'm ready."

Chapter Fifty

MARLOW

ZED GRABBED a marker and scribbled on my cast: *get better soon you big idiot.*

"You really have a way with words," I said, reading it upside down. "You should work for Hallmark."

It'd been awkward between us since he started dating Dakota, but I'd also started dating Sage. Almost dying reminds a person what's important and what's just... not.

"Hey," I started as Zed settled back on his bed, "I want you to know, I'm fine with you dating my ex-girlfriend. In fact, I'm happy for you."

"Is that the painkillers talking?"

"I'm only on Tylenol now."

Relief washed over Zed's hairy face. "Thanks for telling me. It means a lot."

"Sure. Dakota was right when she said we'd do better as friends."

"So, you won't be weirded out to see me with her?"

"I mean, yeah, it's kind of weird, but it's early. A month from now, I'm sure things will be different."

"Dakota's okay with you being with Sage too. She just wants you to be happy."

"You've landed a very cool girl, my friend," I said.

He laughed. "I know. I should probably thank you for dating her first. I might not have met her otherwise."

I checked the time, grabbed my crutch and hopped my way across the room.

"Hot date with Sage?" Zed said, his dark brows jumping as he teased.

"You could say that."

Sage picked me up in her truck.

"Boy Toy to the rescue," she said as I climbed in.

"Please, please can you stop calling it that. Normal people don't name their vehicles."

She leaned in to kiss me. "You better than anyone should know I'm not normal."

"True," I said, keeping my lips on hers. "But if you must name it, can you please pick something else?"

She laughed as she pulled away from me and shifted into gear. "What should I call it then?"

"Bob?"

"Fine." She ran her hand over the dusty dash. "I now christen you Bob."

All traces of Harland and his killing spree would soon be erased from our minds. When the tower crashed in the cellar, the teleportation system crashed with it. Harland Payne's brains were so fried from his repeated use of the technology that he couldn't remember how to set it up again.

Jack had given us the address of CISUE since we were going to leave without remembering any of it anyway.

Sage drove into the parking area underneath the nondescript building and claimed a spot. I took her hand. "Are you ready for this?"

She shrugged. "It's not like we haven't done this before."

The room Jack took us to was small and window-less, and reminded me of a clinic where you get x-rays, except instead of an x-ray machine there was a chair with a sci-fi looking upside-down bowl with wires hanging from it.

Agent Kato was there, in an even smaller adjoining room that was divided from this one by a Plexiglas wall. She wore a white lab coat and cat-eye glasses, and was tapping something into a machine on the counter.

We'd agreed to play it cool in front of Jack and the CISUE team. We wanted to keep our new relationship safe from scrutiny and judgments.

"Take off your shoes, belts and jewelry," Agent Kato said when she saw us, obviously a get-things-done type. Who needs social niceties? "Coins too. Anything with metal."

"I feel like I'm at the airport," Sage said.

"Do you want to go first?" I asked with a smile. I couldn't stop myself from bumping up against her arm. "I'll meet you on the other side."

She nibbled on her bottom lip, and I worried she might buck my suggestion, but then she agreed. "Okay."

I gave her hand a quick squeeze before taking a spot beside Jack and Agent Kato in the adjoining room.

Dr. Turner applied wired patches to Sage's temples and the base of her neck, and secured the bowl onto her head. He looked wistful as he said, "You won't remember me after this, so I'm going to say my good-byes now. Goodbye, Sage."

"Goodbye, Dr. Turner."

Kato turned on the unit from behind the glass. Sage searched for me and held my gaze for a moment before closing her eyes.

"What's going on with you two?" Jack said, annoying me with his secret agent perceptiveness skills.

"Nothing."

"Nothing my ass." He chuckled. "You made a move on her, didn't you?"

Heat flashed up my neck and I cursed my inability to stay cool like I'd intended.

"Maybe."

He patted me on the back. "That's my boy."

It felt good to be affirmed and admired by my dad. *My dad*. I rarely referred to him like that, especially to myself.

"How long does it take to complete the memory wipe?"

Agent Kato answered, "Twelve minutes."

Pretty precise, and how long I had to make my case. I pulled Jack and Dr. Turner to the side.

"I want to renegotiate."

Dr. Turner raised a graying brow. "What do you mean?"

"I don't want to have my memories erased."

Jack clucked. "You agreed, Marlow."

"I know, but what about the next time something strange happens? And statistically speaking, you have to agree, there will be a next time. I don't know why Sage and I are always pulled in, but we are. I need to have my wits about me. How can I protect her if I don't know what's going on?"

Jack and Dr. Turner shared a look, like they knew the answer to why Sage and I constantly found ourselves in the middle of the unusual, but they weren't talking. My eyes darted to Sage, her expression peaceful as if sleeping.

"He has a point," Dr. Turner finally said. "Sage's safety is paramount."

"I'm partial to Marlow staying alive too," Jack said.

"Of course," Dr. Turner said. "But doesn't it make sense that he would be better equipped to do that if he were on watch?"

There was a quiet series of pings, like the microwave telling you your food is ready. Agent Kato approached Sage and began to remove the cap and wires.

"You'll have to act like you know nothing about CISUE," Jack said, "or the details of this last incident."

"I will," I said.

Dr. Turner nodded in agreement, then slipped outside before Sage woke up.

Jack gave me a look: part "be careful" and part "be careful with *her*."

Agent Kato led Sage out to a recovery room and I waited a few minutes before joining her. "Are you ready to go?"

"What are we doing here, Marlow?" she asked. "No one will tell me anything."

"Jack brought us here, but now we have to leave."

"But why?"

"I'm not sure. Jack said he'd tell us later."

It was a good thing that Sage trusted Jack. It felt wrong to mislead her like this, but it was for her own safety. I wondered what Jack would've told me if I'd gone through with it? Made up some plausible reason, likely.

Sage appeared lightheaded, and I hoped she hadn't forgotten *everything*. I'd kill Jack if she didn't remember the "us" that had begun only twenty-four hours earlier. She walked with me as I hobbled on my crutch to the black sedan that waited to take us back to campus, and I ushered her into the back seat.

Once the doors were closed and our driver had us on our way, she turned to me and smiled, a flirtatious glint in her eyes. I exhaled and a load of worry dropped off my shoulders.

I cupped her head pulling her close and whispered in her ear, "Now where were we?"

If you enjoyed reading *Twinkle Little Star* please help others enjoy it too.

Recommend it: Help others find the book by recommending it to friends, readers' groups, discussion boards and by suggesting it to your local library.

Review it: Please tell other readers why you liked this book by reviewing it at Amazon or Goodreads. If you do write a review, Let me know at leestraussbooks@gmail.com so I can thank you.

Visit www.leestraussbooks.com and get Lee's starter library - FREE!

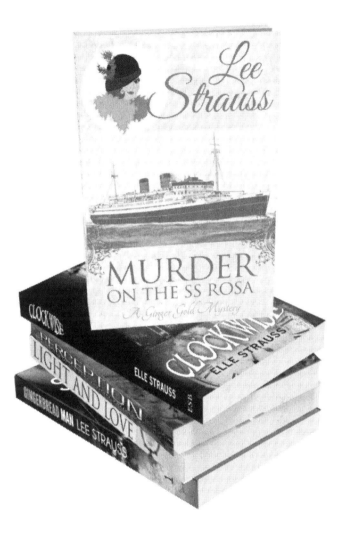

MY NEWEST SERIES is the **Ginger Gold Mystery** series, cozy historical mysteries set in 1920s

England. If you're a fan of authors who wrote while living in that era such as Agatha Christie and Dorothy L. Sayers, or contemporary authors who set their stories in the early 20th century like Rhys Bowen and Frances Brody, you're sure to like Ginger Gold!

1920S FASHIONISTA GINGER GOLD puts her wartime operative skills to work in the Jazz Age!

In the spirit of Agatha Christie, Lee Strauss presents a brand new series reminiscent of the Golden Age of Mysteries.

Murder's a pickle.

It's 1923 and young war widow fashionista Ginger Gold makes a cross-Atlantic journey with her companion Haley Higgins to London England to settle her father's estate. When the ship's captain is found dead, Ginger is only too happy to lend her assistance to the handsome Chief Inspector Basil Reed.

The SS Rosa delivers a convincing array of suspects—the wife, the mistress, a jealous crew mate. To Ginger's dismay, her name has been added to the list! With a little help from Ginger's dog Boss, Ginger and Haley navigate the clues (those wartime operative skills come in handy.) They must solve the case and clear Ginger's name before they dock—and oh, whatever shall she wear!

GET IT ON AMAZON

About the Author

Lee Strauss is the bestselling author of the Ginger Gold Mysteries series (cozy historical mysteries), a Nursery Rhyme Mystery series (mystery, sci-fi, young adult), the Perception Trilogy (YA dystopian mystery), the Light & Love series (sweet romance) and young adult historical fiction. When she's not writing or reading, she likes to cycle, hike, and kayak. She loves to drink caffè lattes and red wines in exotic places, and eat dark chocolate anywhere.

Lee also writes younger YA fantasy as Elle Lee Strauss.

For more info on books by Lee Strauss and her social media links, visit leestraussbooks.com. To make sure you don't miss the next new release, be sure to sign up for her readers' list.

www.leestraussbooks.com

Books by Lee Strauss

Ginger Gold Mysteries (cozy historical)

*Cozy. Charming. Filled with Bright Young Things. This Jazz
Age murder mystery will entertain and delight you with its
1920s flair and pizzazz!*

Murder on the SS *Rosa*

Murder at Hartigan House

Murder at Bray Manor

Murder at Feathers & Flair

Murder at the Mortuary

Murder at Kensington Gardens

Murder at St. Georges Church

Murder aboard the Flying Scotsman

A Nursery Rhyme Suspense (mystery/sci fi)

*Marlow finds himself teamed up with intelligent and savvy
Sage Farrell, a girl so far out of his league he feels blinded in*

her presence - literally - damned glasses! Together they work to find the identity of @gingerbreadman. Can they stop the killer before he strikes again?

Gingerbread Man

Life Is but a Dream

Hickory Dickory Dock

Twinkle Little Star

The Perception Trilogy (YA dystopian mystery)

Zoe Vanderveen is a GAP—a genetically altered person. She lives in the security of a walled city on prime water-front property along side other equally beautiful people with extended life spans. Her brother Liam is missing. Noah Brody, a boy on the outside, is the only one who can help ∼ but can she trust him?

Perception

Volition

Contrition

Light & Love (sweet romance)

Set in the dazzling charm of Europe, follow Katja, Gabriella,
Eva, Anna and Belle as they find strength, hope and love.

Sing me a Love Song

Your Love is Sweet

In Light of Us

Lying in Starlight

Playing with Matches (WW2 history/romance)

A sobering but hopeful journey about how one young Germany
boy copes with the war and propaganda. Based on true events.

As Elle Lee Strauss

The Clockwise Collection (YA time travel romance)

Casey Donovan has issues: hair, height and uncontrollable
trips to the 19th century! And now this ~ she's accidentally
taken Nate Mackenzie, the cutest boy in the school, back in
time. Awkward.

Clockwise

Clockwiser

Like Clockwork

Counter Clockwise

Clockwork Crazy

Standalones

Seaweed

Love, Tink

Acknowledgments

A big thank you to the fans of A NURSERY RHYME MYSTERY series! You are the best.

I have to shout out to my editor Angelika Offen-wanger for always keeping me on course, to Steven Novak for another great cover, and to my early readers and review team - Thank you!

47671177R00177

Made in the USA
Lexington, KY
10 August 2019